T0063475

Prescription for Revolution

Thomas H. Lee

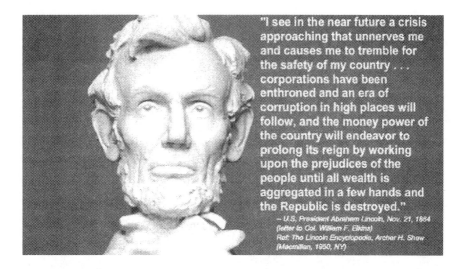

"I see in the near future a crisis approaching that unnerves me and causes me to tremble for the safety of my country . . . corporations have been enthroned and an era of corruption in high places will follow, and the money power of the country will endeavor to prolong its reign by working upon the prejudices of the people until all wealth is aggregated in a few hands and the Republic is destroyed."

– U.S. President Abraham Lincoln, Nov. 21, 1864
(letter to Col. William F. Elkins)
Ref: The Lincoln Encyclopedia, Archer H. Shaw
(Macmillan, 1950, NY)

Isn't it amazing that Lincoln, in addition to his other remarkable leadership qualities, was so prophetic regarding the Union's future. Unfortunately his fears and concerns expressed to Colonel Elkins in 1864 and echoed by President Eisenhower in 1959 have come to pass. Powerful corporations and wealthy conservatives, fronted by the corrupt Republican Party, now control the federal government. They control it to the extent that the wealthiest 1 percent in this country has amassed more than 25 percent of our national wealth. This obscene maldistribution of wealth is slowly but surely impoverishing our middle and working classes and undermining our democracy. But what can be done about it?

The novel you are about to read answers that question.

Prescription for Revolution

A Sequel

INTRODUCTION

▼

Those of you who have recently read *A Quiet Revolution* may skip this introduction. It is intended for those unfamiliar with that prequel.

The prequel, *A Quiet Revolution*, tells the story of five individuals who, upon seeing a cancer of corruption growing on America's democracy, agree to a dangerous collaboration to help remove it. The five, thinking of themselves as phantom patriots, develop and execute a plan to eliminate the worst of the corruptors. Their quiet revolution succeeds in bringing down a conservative Republican administration that, while singularly engaged in enriching themselves and their powerful benefactors, brought this country to the brink of financial disaster.

When we last heard from the five, they were celebrating having succeeded in helping put a Democrat in the White House. However, it soon became clear that even though they had won the battle, they were not winning the war. In the sequel you are about to read, the phantom patriots develop and execute a comprehensive strategy to reform the government and restore democracy to the American people.

To set the stage, let me introduce you to the five phantom patriots. They first became associated while serving in Vietnam in various black ops and intelligence capacities. They were most closely associated during the frenetic and dangerous months leading up to the fall of Saigon on April 30, 1975.

The most senior of the group, John Harrison, was then director of field operations for the CIA in Vietnam. His cover name in that capacity was Lawrence Green. Green controlled over six hundred field agents. The second of the phantom patriots was Green's attractive secretary/executive assistant, Jennifer Olson. Jennifer, ten years Green's junior, was also a career officer in the CIA's Clandestine Service. They later married.

The third patriot in this story was then an air force lieutenant colonel named Terry Lawson, who at the time was assigned to the US Joint Service Command (USSAG) in Thailand with responsibility for all computer-based information systems in Southeast Asia. In February 1975 he was sent to the defense attaché's office in Saigon to correct and enhance a number of intelligence reporting systems belonging to a GS-15 named Larry Green (a.k.a. John Harrison). Lawson and his people were able to make significant improvements in Green's intelligence systems, but unfortunately it was too little too late.

The fourth phantom patriot, Jack Hanley, was at the time an air force major that Lawson had met soon after his arrival at USSAG. Hanley was the chief intelligence analyst for USSAG's chief of staff and J-2, Army Major General Ira Hunt. It was Hanley who first called Lawson's attention to the fact that many of Hunt's classified operational reports being sent to the US Military Command Center in the Pentagon were highly inaccurate. Knowing that, Lawson took it upon himself to correct the reports. Throughout Lawson's tour at USSAG, Hanley kept him informed of highly classified back-channel intelligence, as well as black ops and various classified USSAG operations. With mutual respect for one another, Hanley and Lawson became good friends. After the fall of Saigon, both were assigned to the Defense Intelligence Agency in Washington, where they continued their close working relationship. Shortly after the two arrived at DIA headquarters, they were recruited by John Harrison to join the CIA. Both did so but retained their air force identities and careers. After retiring from the air force, both were given full-time jobs at CIA headquarters—Lawson in the science and technology division, Hanley in the agency's counterintelligence division. Over the years both eventually rose to the top of their respective divisions.

The fifth phantom patriot was initially known to Lawson only as the civilian who occasionally occupied the bedroom trailer behind his in Thailand. That individual, in his early thirties, had the distinction of possessing the only civilian vehicle on the large base—a Toyota Corolla. The man, known to Lawson as Al Carpenter, later proved to be a CIA field agent who spent most of his time in Bangkok, coordinating black operations with Thai intelligence. Carpenter carried a plasticized card that directed everyone in the Thai government to give him whatever assistance or resources he requested. The order was signed by the king of Thailand. Carpenter, on his occasional visits to USSAG, provided intelligence reports directly to General Hunt. After the fall of Saigon, Carpenter morphed into Phil Martin and eventually became John Harrison's deputy at CIA headquarters. When Harrison resigned as director of the CIA's Clandestine Service, Phil Martin replaced him.

The story of the five phantom patriots began when they gathered at the Harrisons' retirement home ostensibly to acknowledge the thirtieth anniversary of Saigon's fall, an occasion they were all dramatically involved in. In reality the meeting was a call to arms. During that first intense secret conclave, the five agreed that the incumbent Republican administration, along with its wholly owned Congress, were functioning exclusively to benefit special interests and powerful corporations. Among the beneficiaries of this corruption were Big Oil, defense industry corporations, and gun manufacturers. In that first meeting, the five concurred that America's democracy was in serious jeopardy and that immediate action by them was imperative. And thus a quiet revolution was launched.

And with that as background, it's now time for you to join the phantom patriots who have again gathered at the Harrison's safe-house-like residence, which is located an hour or so south of Washington, DC. The Japanese-style house, situated on three and a half acres, is hidden in a cluster of trees along the banks of the Rappahannock River. It is the patriot's first meeting since the national election of 2012. The meeting was called by John Harrison to assess the status of their quiet revolution. Please join them now.

CHAPTER 1

▼

John Harrison, clearly agitated, was the first to speak. "What the hell went wrong? The president and vice president worked their butts off to win reelection but weren't rewarded with a congressional majority. Job one for the Democrats in that election was to purge every damn obstructionist Republican from Congress. How was it possible for any of those Tea Party clowns to get reelected?"

Lawson raised a finger and said, "Assuming that's not a rhetorical question, John, the answer is 'a combination of things.'"

Harrison drummed his fingers on the table and said, "Please enlighten me."

Lawson wrinkled his brow. "As I just said, it was a multiplicity of things. First of all, the Republicans had a ton of money—a billion three hundred thousand to be exact. Three hundred and fifty million of that came from the Koch brothers. These are the guys that instituted and financed the Tea Party in 2010 and again in this election. With the extravagant help of the brothers, Republicans had such a huge war chest they were able to continuously saturate the conservative news media with lies and propaganda. The effect of that media blitz was that the public was kept ignorant and frightened. But that's just a part of the problem. Remember, a majority of our congressional candidates were running for the first time and were clueless as to how to conduct a winning campaign. The fault here is that the Democratic leadership didn't provide them and their campaign managers with any effective guidance. I chalk that up to the fact those political fossils have little understanding of how to win an election in this modern era. Unfortunately, they've demonstrated that fact over and over again, but never more evidently than in recent years. We had a slam dunk opportunity to win both the White House and Congress in 2000 and 2004 but failed miserably both times. Obviously the Democratic leadership—the DNC and the DCCC—didn't learn a damn thing from those two fiascos and continue to flounder."

Harrison frowned. "What should they have learned from those previous screwups?"

"A very fundamental thing—that negative campaigning, at least the way they do it, simply doesn't work. In fact, it's counterproductive."

Harrison's frown deepened. "What are they doing wrong?"

Lawson smiled. "The wrong way is to denigrate your opponent by name. And why is that wrong? It's simple. When voters enter their polling place, they have only one piece of information to work with, which is a name. And if the name they hear repeatedly during the campaign is that of the Republican candidate, that's the name that'll be lodged in their memory and the one they'll vote for. Simply put, personal negative ads are free advertising tor the opposition candidate. It's inherently counterproductive because positive name recognition by voters is essential to winning an election."

"And the right way is . . . ?"

"That should be obvious. No Dem candidate or supporter should ever refer to the Republican opponent by name. Any reference to the opposition candidate should simply be 'my opponent,' or 'my Republican opponent.' And when appropriate, as 'my Tea Party opponent.'"

Harrison nodded. "You make it sound pretty simple. Why doesn't the Dem leadership understand this?"

It was Lawson's turn to shake his head and frown. "God only knows. What's especially galling to me is that I provided both the DNC and the DCCC with a guidance paper for our candidates. It spelled out step-by-step what they needed to do to defeat their Republican opponents. Unfortunately neither of those organizations acknowledged receipt of my paper, and it wasn't distributed."

Harrison shook his head. "What do you think the problem is?"

Lawson rolled his eyes. "I can only speculate. My guess, however, is that both organizations, which are headed by traditional professional politicians, still cling to the misconception that old-fashioned negative campaigning works. It seems to be a case of not being able to teach old dogs new tricks. My personal complaint is that both organizations wasted my donated money on negative ads vilifying the Republican candidate by name without ever mentioning the name of the Dem running against him or her."

Harrison drummed his fingers on the table. "This is disgusting. Should we expect a repeat of that incompetence in 2014?"

"I would assume so, unless of course we're proactive in educating both the leadership and the candidates. I think my paper would accomplish that objective. It's straightforward and starts with the basics. First it reminds candidates that there are only two reasons voters go to the polls and that's because they're either angry or afraid. So my advice to progressive candidates is that they develop a list of all the reasons voters should be pissed off, and then a similar list of what they should fear."

Harrison nodded. "That seems simple enough. What other advice do you have?"

"The first thing I would tell them is that they should present themselves as the ideal candidate—one who doesn't need the job and is running for all the right reasons, and is beholden to no one. Then I would advise them that they need to understand that Republicans are generally supported by the mainstream media, so they need to take their campaigns directly to the people. And that they can do this effectively at any public gathering or town hall meetings. I would emphasize this last point by reminding candidates that this is exactly what the president and vice president did to win their elections in 2008 and 2012."

Harrison nodded, looked around the table, and said, "That makes good sense. Now how do we convince the Democratic leadership they should embrace and disseminate Terry's guidance?"

Hanley pushed his glasses back and said, "Without being too crass, I would suggest we do it the same way the Godfather would have—we'll make them an offer they can't refuse. We subtly tell them they have a choice—that they can do what we ask, or we'll air out all their dirty laundry."

Harrison smiled. "Well, it's a proven way of getting things done."

Hanley nodded. "No question about it. It'll work because there isn't a single member of Congress that doesn't have something to hide. Since the leadership has been parked on Capitol Hill a long time, they're bound to have a nice collection of compromising things they'd prefer remain private. My guys can easily ferret out all their crap."

Phil Martin smiled and said, "Hell, why go to all that trouble. All we need to do is dig up J. Edgar's files. He had a priceless collection of compromising information on every senior government official in Washington." After pausing for a moment he added, "But knowing Hoover's paranoia, he probably destroyed those files years ago."

Lawson frowned. "Okay, let's get serious. The next election is barely a year away. That means we need to begin preparations immediately to oust every damn obstructionist Republican from Congress. Obviously it'll be a big job, so we need a comprehensive strategic plan soonest."

Jessica Harrison raised a finger and said, "That's true. So how do you propose to jump-start this ambitious operation?"

Lawson nodded, "The way we always have for any operation. That means defining the mission and compiling a list of all the objectives that must be satisfied to accomplish it. After that, we identify the challenges to be resolved in order to achieve the objectives. Then we establish a comprehensive strategic plan containing a set of tactical plans to resolve challenges and accomplish all the objectives."

Harrison nodded. "That sounds familiar." After turning to Martin he asked, "Phil, do you still have access to the black financial resources we spirited out of Vietnam?"

Martin smiled and said, "Of course, and they've recently appreciated significantly. The gold from Saigon has increased in value by more than 40 percent, making it worth somewhere around eight hundred million. In addition we have all the dirty money we drained from the Big Oil guys. So we have enough money to support any type operation you decide on."

Harrison smiled, turned to Lawson, and said, "Terry, that means you can develop as ambitious a plan as you think is needed. When can you start?"

Lawson drew back his head in surprise. "Hold on, John, I just told you what needs to be done. I didn't volunteer to do it."

Martin chuckled and said, "Come on, Terry, since you so succinctly described what needs to be done, you've earned the honor of putting your planning genius where your mouth is."

Hanley raised his hand and said, "I agree with Phil. It's obvious this is Terry's baby."

Unable to hide a smile, Harrison said, "That settles it. Terry, you've got the job."

Lawson frowned. "It's strange, but I feel like I've just been the recipient of a rectal exam."

Jennifer laughed. "That's a personal problem. Obviously you're the most qualified to do this job. Hell, you've been developing operations' plans of one kind or another all your life. Besides, you've covered most of the issues we have to deal with in your op-ed and commentary pieces for the *Post*."

Lawson shook his head. "Would it make any difference if I were to point out I got generously compensated for that ball-busting work?"

In unison the Harrisons and Martin said, "No." Hanley said, "Hell no."

Harrison raised his hand to quiet the muttering. "Terry has proven himself a true patriot on many occasions, and at this moment the stakes have never been higher. And since the very future of our country depends on whether we can successfully clean up the corruption in our government and return democracy to the people, we have to imagine it's the Fourth of July, 1776, all over again."

Lawson looked down at the table and quietly said, "There you go, John, playing the patriot card again. Let's be clear, I'm no Thomas Jefferson or Patrick Henry, but screw it, I'll take the damn job. We can talk about compensation later."

Jennifer clapped and said, "*Merci beaucoup*, Terry. If you come through for us on this, we'll see that you get a guided tour through the White House. Now, on a serious note, I suggest you recruit Lan to help. As you know, she's smart and has proven herself to be a very effective covert agent. She'll be a good sounding board for you. Oh, and she just might give you some compensation the form of extra 'home cooking.'"

Lawson sighed, rolled his eyes, and said, "There's no question Lan will jump at the chance to join our little revolution. But as for the 'home cooking,' I already have as much of that as I can handle."

The other four just smirked. After a moment, Jennifer said, "Good for you, Tiger. I hope you won't be too worn out to generate our plan."

Lawson shook his head and made an obscene gesture.

Before anyone else could speak, Harrison said, "That's enough levity for now. Let's wrap up this meeting. The only piece of business remaining is to set a date for our next meeting. Terry, when do you think you'll have a draft plan for us to review?"

Lawson thought for a few seconds and said, "No more than two weeks."

Jennifer nodded. "Good. The next meeting is tentatively set for two weeks from today. I'll be in contact to confirm the date and time."

Harrison smiled, rapped the table with his knuckles, and said, "Good work, all. Meeting adjourned."

CHAPTER 2

▼

As Lawson drove toward his house in McLean, a wave of exhaustion began to engulf him. He glanced at his watch and saw that it was 2315. It had taken him more than an hour to return from the Harrisons' safe house. He clicked the garage door opener and a few seconds later pulled his black Lexus in alongside Lan's Jaguar. He retrieved his briefcase from the passenger seat and entered the house through a combination mudroom and atrium. Lawson spent a couple moments ensuring that the plants had been watered before going into the adjacent kitchen. When he stepped through the door, he was greeted by Lan, dressed only in a filmy negligee. The negligee concealed nothing of her near-perfect body.

She greeted him in French, saying, "Bonsoir, mon Cheri. C'est une bonne affair, ce soir, n'est pas?"

Lawson grinned, hugged her, and gave her a deep kiss before saying, "God, you look absolutely ravishing. I was about to tell you that we had a good reunion, and that I was *tres fatigue*. But now I feel completely recovered."

Lan laughed. "I certainly hope so. I have plans for tonight."

Lawson nodded. "Good. I was hoping that would be the case. But before we get to that, I have something serious to discuss with you."

Looking surprised, Lan said, "What could possibly be so serious?"

"The affair I was at tonight was actually a rather intense meeting."

Lan cocked her head. "Tell me about it."

"It'll take a few minutes to do that, so let's move to the den. You grab a bottle of Meursault and some cheese while I go upstairs and change. I'll meet you in the den in a couple minutes."

Lan smiled, winked, and said, "Don't linger, *cherie*. I still have plans."

Lawson smiled and winked before disappearing. Lan checked the refrigerator's cheese drawer and found an unopened package of Saint André, one of Lawson's favorites. After plating the cheese and locating a package of rice crackers, she got two wineglasses and took everything into the den. After arranging things on the cocktail table, she went downstairs to their combination recreation room and wine cellar. After a minute or so of looking through their 750-bottle climatically controlled walnut wine cabinet, she found a 2009 Meursault. She uncorked it and took it back up to the den.

She had just begun filling the wineglasses when Lawson returned and said, "Good job, sweetheart." He then kissed her on the cheek and lowered himself onto the couch next to her. He picked up his wineglass, swirled the wine a bit to release the aromas, and then smelled it. He then took a small sip, nodded his approval, and then downed a substantial gulp before saying, "As for the meeting tonight, it was a reunion of sorts but not what I led you to believe. I did meet with the Harrisons, Phil Martin, and Jack Hanley for a reunion, but in reality we met to resume an operation we started four years ago."

Lan nodded. "I suspected as much. So what's the nature of the operation you're engaged in?"

Lawson took a deep breath before responding, "Our operation has the grand purpose of restoring democracy to the American people. The reason I can tell you this now is that you've been invited to join us."

With a skeptical look, Lan said, "Why now?"

"The simplistic answer is, because we need your help. You weren't previously invited because John and the others thought it too dangerous for you, because what we're engaged in would be considered treason by many. And we didn't want you taking that risk."

Lan nodded. "I understand. But that risk didn't stop you, so why should it stop me?"

Lawson smiled. "Good question, my dear. The answer is that the rest of us are older than you. We've had our hour on the stage, but you're still relatively young and have much of your life ahead of you."

Lan shook her head. "Obviously you've found a way to avoid being exposed. I'm sure I can do the same."

Lawson nodded. "There's no doubt of that, since we operate much the same as we all did at the agency—completely in the dark."

"Then it's a nonissue. How can I help?"

Lawson smiled. "I suspect in many ways, but your initial assignment begins in the morning."

Looking startled, Lan said, "So soon . . . and in what capacity?"

Lawson smiled. "You'll be helping me develop a strategic plan for the second phase of our quiet revolution."

Lan remained silent for several moments. She then cleared her throat and spoke slowly. "You and I are going to develop a plan to save the free world? What drug user decided that?"

"Long story short, the decision was made by a consensus of the phantom patriots earlier this evening. Their decision was based on the fact that I've had extensive experience in planning operations. And after that decision was taken, Jennifer suggested you would be an asset in helping me. She's under the impression we work well together."

Lan smiled. "We do, but not in planning—just in doing. And that reminds me, it's been a couple days since we've done anything."

Lawson laughed. "Jennifer also suggested you'd be so grateful at being invited to join our enterprise and being able to help me that you might very well express your gratitude by treating me to more frequent sex. She referred to it euphemistically as 'home cooking.'"

Lan laughed. "How did you respond to that?"

Lawson shrugged his shoulders. "I mentioned that I was getting as much 'home cooking' as I could handle. By the way, what's that perfume you're wearing?"

"Miss Dior. Can I infer from your question that you have some interest in a little home cooking now?"

"That would be correct. Are you ready to whip up a little something?"

Lan laughed. "Allow me to quote a former vice presidential candidate by saying, 'You betcha.' Will you need a blue pill as an appetizer?"

Lawson smiled. "Dear, all you have to do is slip out of that negligee and the Little Soldier will be at full attention. However, to ensure he stays that way for a while, I'll take one."

"*Tres bien, mon Cherie*. While you're getting comfortable and downing a pill, I'll bring the wine and cheese up to the bedroom. I'm sure we can find an innovative way to consume our midnight snack."

Lawson laughed. "I already have some ideas. Meet you in the bedroom in forty-five seconds."

Lan smiled, then lapsed into a May West impression saying, "Take your time, big boy, we've got all night."

CHAPTER 3

▼

Lawson rolled over, rubbed his eyes, and glanced at the bedside clock. It was 0620—twenty minutes later than normal. He attributed the lateness to the fact that it was well past the witching hour when he and Lan finished making love. Lawson smiled as he remembered how delicious that midnight snack had been. *I'm a very lucky man*, he thought. Then, being careful not to wake Lan, he swung his legs off the bed and quietly stood up. He then moved silently into the master bath, shutting the door and turning on the light before washing his hands and splashing cool water on his face. After toweling off, he continued into his walk-in closet to don slippers and a bathrobe. He then returned to the bathroom, turned off the light, and slipped quietly through the bedroom. After descending the stairs to the entry foyer, he swung around and navigated his way to the kitchen. Once there, he turned on the drip coffeemaker Lan had prepared the night before.

As soon as the pot made gurgling noises, Lawson retraced his steps to the front door and went out into the chilly morning air. He quickly retrieved his *Washington Post* and hurried back indoors. After returning to the kitchen, he unfolded the paper, extracted the Sports Section, and laid the other sections on the kitchen table. Before digging into the Sports Section, however, he glanced at the still-dripping coffeemaker. After a minute or so of intensely employing his psychokinetic powers, the pot made a last desperate gurgle and went silent. Lawson immediately poured himself a cup and took a seat at the table.

Then, as he had done every morning for years, Lawson went to the *Post*'s Sports Section, desperately hoping to find any kind of explanation for the Redskins' annual fold-up and early departure from the play-offs. He had been a season ticket holder for more than twenty years and desperately sought some glimmer of hope that the Skins would be a contender next season. He needed something—anything—to justify spending the kind of money his season tickets were costing. But in his gut he reluctantly accepted the fact that he was a football junkie and, as such, would continue to attend Skins' games despite their continuing mediocrity. His only consolation in this annual malaise was that Dallas Cowboys' fans were in pretty much the same depressing boat as him.

When his exhaustive scan of the Sports Section turned up nothing positive regarding the Redskins, Lawson turned his attention to the editorial page. As usual, he checked out the *Post*'s editorial column before reading the commentaries and op-ed pieces. And as usual, he found only one or two of them he agreed with. He dismissed the others as being either uninformed, politically biased, or pure garbage. While continuing to sip his coffee, Lawson skimmed the rest of the paper in an effort to stay abreast of what was happening in Washington. On this day he found little to warrant his attention, so he skipped to the Comics where he would only read three strips. The first of his favorites was Trudeau's *Doonesbury*, which he found to be politically and socially insightful. Next he checked out Thave's *Frank & Ernest*, an exceptionally funny strip of obscure puns. And as usual, he finished by looking at Scott Adams's *Dilbert*, which he viewed as a dead-on satire of organizational nonsense. When he was done with the comics, Lawson folded up the newspaper, drained the remaining coffee from his cup, and went to his office.

As he had done every morning for the past few years, Lawson sat at his desk and began recording his thoughts and intentions. His objective on this particular morning was to establish an agenda to give himself and Lan a structure for developing a plan to guide the second phase of the phantom patriots' revolution. Lawson sensed that most of the pieces of the plan had been wandering around in his head for weeks. The challenge now was to collect those random thoughts and record them in an organized and coherent way. He expected Lan, as she always did, to bring out the best in him. He was confident she would be the catalyst he needed to get the job done.

It was shortly past 0730 when Lan, dressed in an opaque flowered dressing gown, poked her head into Lawson's office and said, "Can I come in?"

"Of course, I've been waiting for you. How did you sleep?"

"Very well thanks to you and that wonderful sleeping pill you gave me."

Lawson laughed. "It was my pleasure. Now then, since you've had a good night's sleep, can I assume you're energized and ready to become a master planner?"

Lan shook her head. "Hardly, you're the master planner. But I expect to be of some help . . . after I've had a little breakfast. Our session last night left me with a bit of an appetite. How about you, are you up for some ham and eggs this morning?"

"You bet. Make that two over easy with one slab of ham and an English muffin."

"Got it," she said. "Give me about fifteen minutes,"

Lawson smiled. "I'll be ready when you are . . . as always."

When breakfast was finished and the kitchen cleaned up, the Lawsons retired to the master suite to ready themselves for the day ahead. After showering together, the two went to their respective walk-in closets to don comfortable clothes. They knew it would be a long and tiring day. Getting started on any extensive project is somewhat like overcoming the inertia of a stationary locomotive. However, both had done it before and knew what to expect.

After picking up cups of coffee from the kitchen, the two repaired to Terry's office. While Lawson settled into the leather executive chair behind his desk, Lan did the same in a matching leather wingback that faced the desk. Lawson was the first to speak. "I've sketched out an agenda to get us started. We have a couple weeks to deliver the plan to the Harrisons, but I want us to have a preliminary draft in seven days. Is that copacetic with you?"

Lan laughed. "If I knew what 'copacetic' meant, I'd probably say yes. As it is, my answer is maybe. Oh, by the way, can I assume Phil will not be giving me any assignments until we finish the plan?"

"Yes, you may."

"Then I'm ready to go."

Lawson smiled. "Okay, to get started I've roughed out an agenda for developing the plan. When we're satisfied with the agenda, we'll go to the top and start fleshing out the skeleton. Okay?"

"Yes, dear. Shall I be the recorder?"

"That would be wonderful, *mon cherie*. You're much better at that sort of thing than I am. We can use our Apple laptops to record notes and compile the final plan."

Lan nodded. "Good idea. That'll give us the flexibility of recording ad hoc information at any time on our iPads and iPhones, which we can upload latter."

Lawson nodded. "That's right. Now, to get things started, I'll put my proposed agenda on the whiteboard to guide our discussions." Lawson then used a black magic marker to write the following:

Define mission
Define objectives
Identify issues related to objectives
Distill facts relevant to objectives
Develop germane findings
Recommend strategy for accomplishing the mission
Develop tactics to achieve objectives and carry out strategy

When he finished, Lawson said, "Does all that make sense to you?"

Lan shook her head. "Defining the mission and objectives, yes, but identifying issues? What's that all about?"

Lawson nodded. "Identifying issues means recognizing the challenges and obstacles that might be encountered while trying to achieve the objectives."

"*Je compris.* And I'm comfortable with the agenda. What's next?"

"Now we define the mission."

Lan smiled. "Since you've been incubating this baby for a while, I presume you have a statement in mind. Is that right?"

"You're right, I do. I think the mission is to reform the government and restore democracy to the American people. Does that work for you?"

Lan nodded. "Yes. It's both comprehensive and comprehensible. It should work for everyone. Now give me a second to record it."

Moments later she looked up and said, "Got it. Now tick off the objectives. I'll interrupt if I don't understand or disagree."

Lawson chuckled. "It's wonderful that all those years of developing a compatible partnership is now paying off. Ready?"

Lan suppressed a smile and said, "Yes, dear. Give them to me slowly so I have enough time to enter them."

Lawson nodded, blew her a kiss, and said, "Objective one is to completely reform Congress. Make a note that this is both a prime and an overarching objective. Until Congress is reformed, none of the other critical reforms can be implemented."

After a few moments of tapping her keyboard, Lan nodded. "I've got it. And now I see what you mean by issues related to the objective. I can tick off a half dozen without even thinking about it."

"Good. But we'll defer getting into that until we have all the objectives recorded. The reason for waiting is that there are numerous interdependencies between objectives, as well as between the challenges associated with those objectives. To keep our planning orderly, we'll continue working top-down. Okay?"

Lan nodded. *D'accord.* This is starting to look a little complicated, so I'm going to record a few notes for future reference."

Lawson smiled. "Good idea. I need to do the same."

For the next several minutes, the Lawsons tapped away at their laptop keyboards. Finally Terry looked up and said, "Ready when you are."

Lan shook her head. "Give me another minute or so."

"No problem. I'll begin shaping up some objectives while I'm waiting."

Lan nodded but said nothing.

The rest of the morning was spent thrashing out comprehensive and lucid objectives. When they broke for lunch, however, they had added just three objectives to their list, which were the following:

** Identify and eliminate, or neutralize, congressional corruptors, e.g., ultra wealthy individuals, senior executives of powerful corporations, special interests, and lobbyists.

** Effect a redistribution of wealth so that the richest 1 percent, who currently own more than 25 percent of the country's wealth, will own no more than 5 percent.
** Reform the completely broken justice system.

After lunch, the Lawsons resumed the task of developing succinct objectives. Their protracted discussion of both the intent and wording of a proposed objective was taking at least thirty minutes. By the end of the day, both realized that fleshing out the plan would not be a simple matter. They managed, however, to add six more objectives:

** Implement needed regulatory reforms to prevent Wall Street firms from inventing fraudulent investment instruments and reaping huge windfall profits from their sale.
** Restore the regulatory capabilities of the FTC, FCC, OMB, and DOE to eliminate the often illegal operations of powerful corporations.
** Overhaul of the federal tax code so that wealthy individuals and excessively profitable corporations are made to pay their fair share of taxes.
** Reduce the Department of Defense's bloated budget by at least 10 percent. Note: For the current budget, that would be around sixty billion dollars.
** Define and clarify the nation's war on terrorism.
** Implement federal laws to restrict the sale and use of guns.

That evening, the Lawsons consumed an entire bottle of a 2005 Cote du Rhone with their dinner. Both were mentally stressed, and the wine worked well as a substitute for unavailable endorphins. After the dinner dishes were washed and put away, they retreated to the den with sizable cups of their favorite Colombian coffee. The next fifteen minutes were spent watching MSNBC and finishing their coffee. Afterward they settled in to watch a Netflix Blu-ray DVD with the first four episodes of the *Homeland* television show. As they watched the highly acclaimed drama, they commented to each other about the quality of the acting and the occasionally authentic dialogue and scenes of CIA counterterrorism operations. Overlooking the occasional discrepancies, they found the show to be highly entertaining.

Four hours later, when the final episode of *Homeland* concluded, the Lawsons dragged themselves upstairs to their bedroom. On the way, Lan said, "No sex tonight, dear. I intend to get about ten hours sleep and won't need a sleeping pill to do it."

Lawson chuckled. "No problem. I'm exhausted too. But I hope this isn't a preview of what the next week will be like. If it is, I may consider resigning and taking you to some tropical paradise where we can get it on whenever we want."

Lan yawned. "That's a pleasant thought, dear, but you know damn well you'll work as long and as hard as you need to produce an effective plan. Now be warned, if you try to wake me at any time during the night, for whatever reason, you run the risk of waking up a eunuch."

Lawson smiled but didn't respond. Minutes later, both were sound asleep.

CHAPTER 4

▼

Two Weeks Later at the Harrisons' House

Lan was greeted by the others as a longtime friend and operational colleague. She had, after all, worked directly for Harrison in Saigon and flew out with him at the end. So as they mingled, drinking champagne, each of them welcomed her as a new member of the team and thanked her for helping Terry develop the plan for the next phase of their quiet revolution. Lan, looking beautiful as ever, expressed her delight at being able to participate in such an important and necessary operation. It was like old times in Saigon.

When the champagne was gone, the group moved quietly to the meeting safe room and went in. Unlike before, there were now six chairs around the oval conference table. In front of the newly added sixth chair was a name holder with a two-by-six strip of rose-colored cardboard. Lan noted there was a similar strip of colored cardboard in front of the other chairs. The one in front of John Harrison's was green; Jennifer Harrison's, brown; Phil Martin's, black; Jack Hanley's, white; and her husband's, gray.

When Harrison noted the quizzical look on her face, he explained, "For operational purposes, we refer to each other by our color name. For instance, I'm Mr. Green, Jennifer is Ms. Brown, and so forth."

Lan smiled and said, "So I'm Ms. Rose and my husband is Mr. Gray. It's a good thing they're compatible colors."

Harrison smiled. "Of course our color names are only used for external communications purposes. With that clarified, let's get this meeting started. Unless someone has something they'd like to discuss, we'll move directly to our only agenda item."

When no one responded, Harrison said, "Terry, the meeting is yours."

Lawson stood up and said, "Thanks, John. My original intent for this evening was to do a PowerPoint presentation of our plan. But I'm not going to do that. Since each of you has a printed copy, you can read it at your leisure. What I am going to do is brief you on the process Lan and I went through to produce it."

Harrison interrupted. "Excuse me, Terry, but what's your purpose in doing that?"

Lawson smiled. "Because the plan we eventually came up with is not what we thought it would be when we started. Shall I continue?"

Harrison nodded. "Please do."

"As I was saying, the planning process Lan and I experienced was quite different than we expected. We started by listing a number of objectives. As soon as we did that, we realized it was in effect a listing of all the things that needed fixing before we could restore democracy to this country. The first objective we listed was to reform Congress. After listing a number of other objectives, we realized that in the main they all depended on a reformed Congress. So reforming Congress is both a prime objective and an overarching objective. Are you with me so far?"

They all nodded.

"Good," Lawson said as he motioned for Lan to project a PowerPoint slide. The slide that appeared on the wall-hung display screen showed ten scattered rectangular boxes, each containing an objective. After giving the others a few moments to look at the slide, Lawson said, "As you can see, each of the boxes contains one of our ten objectives. You can also see that the box for objective one—reforming Congress—is in the middle with the others arrayed around it. This illustrates that reforming Congress is the central and overarching objective in the plan, making it job number one."

Harrison nodded. "That's obvious and clear, Terry. But I'm curious as to why, for instance, fixing our justice system depends on Congress?"

"Good question, John. Lan and I wrestled with that for quite a while. Here's what we came up with. The justice system has devolved into a make-work-for-lawyers institution. When mass murderers like Army Major Nidal Hasan, who was seen to kill thirteen people and wound thirty others, can sit in jail for more than three years awaiting trial—all that time being referred to as 'a suspect'—something is awfully wrong. What the hell is he suspected of? The guy is demonstrably a terrorist and a murdering sociopath. So how is it possible that three and a half years later he hasn't been executed? Unfortunately the answer is pretty obvious. It's just another opportunity to provide jobs for this country's excess of lawyers. In Hasan's case, a significant gaggle of them have been preparing to either prosecute, defend, or judge this terrorist-murderer. But why is it taking so long? Again the answer is simple. The longer it takes to prepare for a completely unnecessary trial, the more fees lawyers can collect. What's especially galling about this agonizingly slow and unnecessary process is that the lawyers will keep muttering the mantra 'No one is guilty until judged so by a jury of his or her peers.' What a crock of baloney. A trial is only needed when there is reasonable doubt. In Hasan's case, he was seen by at least a dozen witnesses to kill or wound forty-three people—there is zero doubt he committed multiple murders. Given that, no trial is needed. The instant that son of a bitch fired his last shot, he was demonstrably guilty of terroristic mass murder and should have been executed at least three years ago. To my way of thinking, he should have been summarily executed at the scene of the crime. But our justice system is completely inverted. It currently functions to serve the guilty while rendering little justice for victims."

Harrison nodded. "You're right, Terry. But that still doesn't answer my question."

"I was getting to that. The purpose of the legal system is to ensure that justice is done, and that lawbreakers are appropriately punished for their crimes. That seems rather straightforward, but it isn't. It's convoluted because the laws that govern the federal justice system are made by Congress, and guess what? A significant number of congressmen are lawyers. And many of them would be chasing ambulances if they didn't have that cushy part-time job that compensates them quite generously with full-time pay. The bottom line here is that we have lawyers making the laws that regulate the federal justice system, which in turn is run by fellow attorneys. The consequence of this professional nepotism is that we now have too many damn lawyers in this country feeding from the trough of a seemingly stagnant justice system. I think Shakespeare had it right when he wrote, 'First kill all the lawyers.' Does that answer your question, John?"

Harrison nodded. "Yes, indeed. Now are you going to talk about the dependency of the other objectives as well?"

"Certainly, and I'll start with 'Clarify the war on terrorism.' Currently we have no coherent program which is both comprehensive and sensible. Simply put, the existing antiterrorist program is convoluted and disjointed. It is based on an often contradictory patchwork of definitions which attempt to spell out both what terrorists are and what an act of terrorism is. The main thrust of our so-called war on terrorism is aimed at identifying and eliminating Middle Eastern Muslim jihadists—people who are outspokenly dedicated to destroying the United States. In my mind this focus is much too narrow and creates too many legal questions. I believe a terrorist is any individual or group that wantonly kills three or more people—period! Motive is irrelevant. And it shouldn't matter whether such an act of terrorism occurs on foreign soil or here in the US. Nor should it matter what country the perpetrator or perpetrators are from. For instance, when an American college student goes into a university or a movie theater and shoots to death a significant number of people, he is a terrorist. He is immediately guilty of a capital crime and should be put to death as quickly as possible. As I said before, motive and state of mind are irrelevant. Therefore, no lawyers need be involved. And the perpetrator should not be allowed to escape the death penalty by pleading guilty. In that same vein, it shouldn't matter if the act of terrorism is committed by jihadists, Mexican drug cartels, or a street gang in Chicago. All participants are equally guilty of murder and deserve to die."

Phil Martin applauded. "Well said, Terry. As you know, it's frustrating for us to hunt and eliminate terrorists in all parts of the world without ruffling the feathers of someone in Congress. I get pretty sick of having to hike over to Capitol Hill every week or two to testify to some phony oversight committee on what we did or didn't do in dealing with terrorists. In most cases the sole purpose of the hearing is for the committee members to score political points for their party. The program you're proposing would make my job a hell of a lot easier—and more effective."

Lawson smiled. "Thanks, Phil. But as you well know, getting such a program legislated depends on cleaning out Congress, which reminds me—I didn't mention political terrorists. Those obstructionist Tea Party clowns are the poster people for political terrorism. Several of those assholes have publicly stated that their only purpose in Washington is to make the government and the president fail. In my mind that makes them anarchists and enemies of the people. If the Alien and Sedition Act were still in effect, all those parasitic numbskulls would be in jail."

Jennifer motioned to speak. "Thanks, Terry. I think we all agree with what you just said regarding the antiterrorism objective. Now tell me about the objective to reform the tax code.'"

Lawson nodded. "Glad to. The current federal tax code is heavily skewed in favor of the ultra wealthy. Very few of the wealthiest 1 percent have much in the way of earned income—the bulk of their income is derived from capital gains, which is currently taxed at the ridiculously low rate of 15 percent. A prime example of this gross injustice is last year's Republican presidential candidate. That aloof and wealthy phony paid only 13 percent in federal income tax. That's less than most low-income blue-collar workers pay. Plain and simple, it's a national disgrace. Now how do we fix this ludicrous situation? You've got it—Congress has to completely revamp the federal tax code."

Harrison nodded. "You've made it rather clear that Congress has to be purged before we can make the wealthy pay their fair share of taxes. But what about the objective 'Effect a redistribution of wealth so that the richest 1 percent own less than 10 percent of the nation's wealth'?"

Lawson smiled. "That one is a bit more complicated and will take longer to achieve. The first step, as just mentioned, is to reform the tax code. The second step is to ensure that the middle and working classes get a substantially greater share of the rapidly expanding corporate profits than they currently do. This can be accomplished by, among other things, raising the minimum wage, implementing profit sharing, and limiting the income for senior corporate executives who are significantly overpaid. Another important step would be to tax excess profits. If that were done, the additional revenue could be plowed back into the economy in the form of public works aimed at repairing our crumbling infrastructure. This would create at least a few million well-paying jobs for both working and middle-class workers."

Harrison smiled. "I agree, Terry. It irritates the hell out of me that a huge corporation like ExxonMobil can report a quarterly profit of sixteen billion dollars without anyone even raising an eyebrow. It's simply obscene. And as you previously pointed out, excess profits indicate that a corporation's products are overpriced. In this case ExxonMobil's huge profits indicate that its primary products, fuels such as gas and oil, are significantly overpriced."

Lawson nodded. "That's exactly right. But again, before anything else can be done, we need a Congress that isn't beholden to ultra wealthy individuals and powerful corporations. I could go over the other objectives, but in each case there is an initial dependency on badly needed and common-sense congressional legislation."

Hanley raised his hand. "Excuse me, Terry, but it seems to me you have one objective that takes precedence over the others."

"Which one are you referring to, Jack?"

"The one that reads, 'Significantly dilute the power of the corruptors.'"

Lawson smiled. "I put that one in for you, Jack. Actually achieving that objective is a two-part task. Your part would involve diminishing their power by siphoning off a significant amount of their wealth. The second part is more complicated. It involves sanitizing Congress to the extent that its members would find it very difficult, and career ending, to take illegal bribes or favors from corporate lobbyists."

Hanley nodded. "I can handle the siphoning part, but sanitizing Congress? That's not likely to happen in my lifetime."

Lawson smiled. "You haven't seen the whole plan yet."

Harrison raised his hand and said, "That's right, Terry. Now what about the issue of gun controls. Do you address that in your plan?"

Lawson nodded. "Yes, but in an abstract way."

"Which is . . . ?"

"As things currently stand, the NRA's well-paid lobbyists ensure that not a shred of gun control legislation will ever be enacted. So I have an alternate plan in mind."

"Which is . . . ?"

"The Second Amendment to the Constitution only addresses the right to bear arms—it's completely silent on the right to own ammunition. So my recommendation is to stimulate a public movement to ban the public sale of ammunition. Under my plan, avid gun owners can own and coddle as many handguns and automatic weapons as they want, they just won't be able to fire them. Under my proposed law, only the federal government will be able to buy ammunition and control the distribution of it. The distribution of ammunition would be, for example, exclusively to the military, law enforcement agencies, licensed gun clubs, and licensed hunters. The unlawful sale or distribution of restricted ammunition would net the offender a ten—to twenty-year jail sentence."

Harrison smiled. "It's a grand plan, Terry, but getting such legislation through Congress wouldn't have a snowball's chance in hell."

"That's probably true, John. But imagine the public backlash against every one of those congressional prostitutes who voted against it. They'd be extremely vulnerable the next time they were up for reelection."

Harrison nodded. "Your point is well taken. Now let's move on. You've given us the foundation for reviewing and understanding the rest of your plan, so now the ball's in our court. I suggest we reconvene in a week to discuss your recommendations. Phil, Jack, does that work for you two?"

Martin nodded. Hanley smiled and said, "I'm a somewhat slow reader, but I compensate for that by reading the ending first. So yeah, I'll be ready in a week."

Harrison nodded, looked around, and said, "Meeting adjourned. Jennifer will contact you to confirm the date and time of the next meeting. We'll try to do it on a Sunday so we'll have an entire day to gain a consensus regarding the recommended plan of action. See you then."

CHAPTER 5

▼

Sunday Morning, Eight Days Later, at the Harrisons' House

When the patriots had finished the brunch Jennifer had prepared, they retired to the meeting safe room. The four visitors, still chatting among themselves, went there with a coffee cup in one hand and a brief case in the other. Jennifer, who preceded them, carried a fresh pot of coffee. Once everyone was seated, Harrison said, "Fill up your coffee cups and get comfortable. I expect this meeting to be a long one. What we're about to embark on will have historical significance, so we need to ensure that all Ts are crossed and Is dotted. Terry will lead the review and subsequent discussion of his proposed plan. Terry."

Lawson stood up and said, "I'm going to kick off this session by presenting an executive summary of the plan to serve as the basis for the subsequent discussion. The format of the executive summary is, in this order: facts, findings, conclusions, and recommendations. Progressively the facts, findings, and conclusions will build the case for the recommendations I'm making to implement our plan. I know I'm preaching to the choir on this, but please bear with me. It's essential we have an agreed-upon foundation for the recommended plans of action. Is that agreeable?"

Phil Martin nodded. "Can I assume you want us to challenge any fact, finding, or conclusion we don't understand or agree with?"

"Of course, that's the idea. In effect what we'll be doing today is marking up the plan as currently written. When we've completed this review and have a consensus on the plan of action, we can discard the foundation rationale and focus on the strategy and tactics to be employed. Are there any other questions?"

Hanley shook his head. "Fire away, Terry."

Lawson nodded to Lan, who brought up the first PowerPoint chart labeled FACTS. The chart listed the following:

The core of the Republican Party is comprised of white male pseudo Christians and is owned and operated by far-right conservatives whose current mission is to have the president fail. In the past two decades, when Republicans controlled Congress, they failed to pass a single piece of legislation benefiting a majority of Americans. In the past two years they have passed the fewest pieces of legislation in congressional history and, as a consequence, have a single-digit approval rating.

It is a combination of ultra wealthy individuals, powerful corporations, and special interests such as the NRA that have corrupted a significant portion of Congress.

The conservative media controls nearly 90 percent of the so-called news dished out to the American public.

##Republican candidates for Congress have nearly unlimited funding for their campaigns.

The conservative and politicized Supreme Court has enabled corporations to donate as much money to conservative PACs as they want. The court has also rescinded many of the voter protection laws, which have ensured minority voters were not discriminated against at election time.

The criminal justice system is badly broken. Enough said.

The number of mass murders committed with the use of automatic weapons is increasing at an alarming rate.

The convoluted federal tax code is both regressive and heavily skewed in favor of the wealthy.

Many federal regulatory agencies, e.g., the FTC, FCC, SEC, and FERC, are hamstrung to the extent that they can no longer effectively perform their regulatory functions.

Many corporations are enjoying excess profits, little if any of which is shared with workers. At the same time, corporate executives are paying themselves excessively high salaries and awarding themselves overly generous bonuses and stock options. On average corporate CEOs make 350 times as much as their employees.

The excess profitability of many corporations is due in part to the fact that each year they collectively receive more than ninety billion dollars in unwarranted corporate welfare.

After a few moments Lawson said, "Any comments on those facts?"

Harrison nodded. "Jennifer and I nitpicked the wording of a couple of them, but I believe the list is sufficiently comprehensive and comprehensible for us to move on. Phil, Jack, what do you two think?"

Both nodded and Hanley said, "I agree. Let's move on."

"Okay, Terry," Harrison said. "Let's see your findings."

Lawson nodded and a slide labeled findings appeared. It displayed the following list:

The primary source of congressional corruption is ultra wealthy individuals, powerful corporations such as Big Oil, and special interests such as the NRA. In most cases their corrupting money is delivered to individual congressmen by well-paid professional lobbyists, many of whom formerly served in Congress.

The absence of regulatory controls has enabled a number of deleterious things to happen. First, conservative media moguls have been able to dramatically expand their news empires. Second, Wall Street investment firms have been able to continue their criminal investment practices. Third, corporate giants are able to merge and monopolize major industries. And last but not least, major corporations are now making excessive profits by grossly overcharging for their products, e.g., the oil companies for fuel.

The broken criminal justice system enables terrorists to evade the death penalty by pleading guilty to an obvious mass murder.

The wealth of the richest 1 percent in this country is growing exponentially. That's due in large part to a lack of federal regulations and highly favorable tax laws.

The Republican Party, through legislative inaction, is responsible for enabling the wealthy to continuing getting wealthier while the country experiences a dangerous deterioration in education, social programs, health care, the nation's infrastructure, and the environment.

Republican-controlled states are busy implementing discriminatory election policies thanks to the Supreme Court's dismantling of the federal Voting Rights Act. Gerrymandering and voter suppression are common practices in red states.

The same Wall Street bandits who, in 2008, plunged this country into a near depression are still free and continue to enrich themselves by selling risky investment vehicles to naive investors. Another Wall Street disaster seems inevitable. The blame for this is the failure of the Justice Department to prosecute Wall Street executives whose criminal actions are known and well documented.

Congress's refusal to pass the most basic of gun control legislation, i.e., common-sense background checks, means that gun violence in this country will worsen. Hundreds of people, including dozens of children, will be killed every year by sociopaths wielding automatic weapons. The United States will continue to lead the world by a large margin in the annual deaths caused by gunshot wounds.

When he had finished reading the list of findings, Harrison said, "I'm extremely agitated, and there's no question we need to act as soon as is practical. But before getting into Terry's recommended plan of action, let's take a fifteen-minute break."

CHAPTER 6

▼

A Short Time Later

When everyone was seated, Lawson signaled for Lan to bring up his recommendations slide. As soon as it appeared, he said, "I'm recommending both a short-term strategy and a long-term strategy, and here's why. Since we recognize that none of the reforms will be enacted by the current Congress, our immediate focus should be to gain a decisive majority in both the House and the Senate in 2014. If we accomplish that, we can expect most of the common-sense reforms so badly needed will be enacted rather quickly. So there's no question we need a near-term strategy to win control of Congress in 2014. But accomplishing that won't be sufficient for us to complete our revolution."

Harrison shook his head. "And why is that?"

Lawson smiled. "Thanks for the setup, John. The reason it won't be sufficient is that the centerpiece of our democracy, the Congress, will remain unreformed. And, as we've said many times, Congress will never reform itself. So we need a long-term strategy that will enable that to happen."

Harrison frowned. "What do you have in mind?"

Lawson smiled. "The only practical way that Congress can be reformed is through a constitutional amendment. What such an amendment would accomplish, among other things, is the establishment of term limits, reducing and fixing salaries, and eliminating all the perks that currently include cushy medical plans and extremely generous retirement packages."

Harrison raised his eyebrows. "I find that interesting, but hardly feasible. How in the hell could we ever get three-quarters of the states to ratify a constitutional amendment?"

Lawson shook his head. "It won't be easy, but it can be done. Remember what Chairman Mao once said, 'A journey of a thousand miles begins with a single step.' Let me explain how we take that first step. In the past, constitutional amendments have been initiated by two-thirds of both houses of Congress. A proposed amendment would then be sent to the states where three-fourths of them would have to ratify it. I agree it would be near impossible to get it done that way. But there's an alternative. The alternative is to have the proposed amendment initiated by the legislatures of two-thirds of the states. In that approach each state legislature would convene a formal constitutional convention to bless the proposed amendment. After that, it would require three-fourths of the states to approve the amendment for it to be implemented."

Jennifer raised a finger and said, "I can't see that the alternative approach would have any greater chance of passing than the first."

Lawson smiled. "It would, and here's why. The essential difference in the two approaches is that in the alternative way Congress is bypassed."

Harrison shook his head. "That's good, but how do we get two-thirds of the states to propose an amendment and then get three-fourths of them to affirm it?"

Lawson thought for a few moments before saying, "Obviously, it will require turning a number of red states blue, and that won't be easy. But I have an idea of how we can lay the groundwork for doing that."

Jennifer wrinkled her brow and said, "I'm dying to hear this."

Lawson smiled. "We can lay the groundwork for turning red states blue while implementing the strategy for retaking Congress in 2014. It'll be a two-step process. First we have to successfully inform the voting public of all that's wrong with the current, Republican-controlled Congress, which has an 8.7 percent approval rating—the worst in history. We need to spell out precisely what the obstructionist Republican Party is costing this nation, as well as them personally. The objective here is to infuriate voters to the extent they'll be motivated to vote our progressives in and, in effect, their conservative Republican opponents out. And we can accomplish that by spreading the word nationwide that this country can no longer afford the Republican Party."

Jennifer interrupted, "Could you explain please?"

Lawson nodded. "Over the past two decades, Republicans have squandered trillions of taxpayers' dollars while debilitating this country in a variety of ways. High on that list is the fact they allowed 9/11 to happen. Then they instigated an unnecessary and hideous unfunded war in the Middle East, which cost us more than five trillion dollars. And as if that wasn't enough, Republicans drove this country into a disastrous recession that cost another five trillion dollars to recover from. Most recently Republicans have shut down the government at a cost of nearly thirty billion dollars. And the litany goes on."

Harrison said, "All that's true, but how do you intend to package that for public consumption?"

Lawson took a deep breath and said, "The most comprehensive and effective way is to have Sidney Thurston write a sequel to his best-selling exposé of Big Oil's political clout in this country. With what we can feed him, he should be able to write another highly charged and revelatory best seller. But that won't be sufficient since too many Americans don't read books. So it's essential that his book makes it onto the big screen where tens of millions can see it. Once a movie is made based on his book, it will be shown all over the country, and legitimate news media such as MSNBC will talk about it and its message. In addition, we can co-opt the social media to help disseminate the facts in his book. Finally, we equip every candidate with the basic narrative that this country can no longer afford the Republican Party, a message we push especially hard in red states."

Jennifer cocked her head. "And how do you propose to implement this strategy?"

Lawson nodded. "The most immediate step, of course, is to get Thurston started on producing a book compelling enough to become a movie. With such a compelling story in wide distribution, it should be easy to entice a leading screenwriter such as Aaron Sorkin to write the screenplay. And with someone of his caliber producing the screenplay, I'm sure a number of leading Hollywood producers would compete to acquire the movie rights. In the margin, if additional production money was needed, we could show up as investors."

Harrison smiled. "I like it. What's Thurston's status now—is he still in a safe house on the Eastern Shore?"

Martin nodded. "Yes and no. We have him set up with two pseudo identities, one of which he uses as the resident of the Eastern Shore safe house. That's where he does his writing. He uses the other identity for anonymous travel outside the US."

"Good," Harrison said. "Can I assume, Terry, you'll be visiting the Eastern Shore sometime soon?

"It would seem so, wouldn't it? And it also seems that when I see him I need to suggest that his new book pick up where the previous one left off. Since it's a sequel, he'll be able to continue exposing the extraordinary power of Big Oil over the government of this country. I'm sure he'll write about how the oil guys buy the legislation they need to continue making obscene profits. And I'm sure he'll explain that those excess profits are the direct result of the oil cartel overcharging for their fuel products. I also expect him to explain the negative impact that such overpricing has on the middle and working classes. I'll suggest he describe how every vehicle owner is paying twice as much for gas as they should be, and that their airline tickets are so expensive because the airline's primary operating expense is overpriced aviation fuel."

Jennifer smiled. "That should take care of the informational aspect of the book, now what about the entertainment part?"

"My idea is that he should lay bare all the warts of the most corrupt of the oil guys, and do the same to all their main political puppets. I have no doubt they all have a bundle of dirty secrets, both sexual and otherwise. Of course, Thurston will need help from us in discovering those lurid facts."

Hanley nodded. "No problem, we'll get whatever he needs. Just let me know."

Harrison nodded. "What's the next step in your implementation strategy, Terry?"

Lawson thought for a moment. "I suggest after we get Thurston up and running that we focus entirely on gaining a congressional majority in 2014. However, in the process of doing that we should also start laying the groundwork for turning red states blue."

Harrison frowned. "And how do you suggest we do that?"

Lawson nodded. "I propose we launch our national campaign to win back Congress in the great state of Texas."

"Why Texas?"

"For several reasons, but mainly because it's Big Oil's principal breeding ground for corrupt politicians such as the Tea Party folks. And it's also vulnerable because in the past decade and a half, under the governorships of dumb and dumber, Texas has maintained its dubious position of being forty-ninth in education, fiftieth in public health, and fiftieth in environment protection. In addition to those reasons, it has one of the worst criminal justice systems in the country. And anyone who doubts this should read John Grisham's novel *The Confession*. And Texas executes more than four times the number of people as any other state. So combine all those reasons and you have to conclude that Texas is a big, slow-moving target. That's why I believe Texas can be turned blue with a well-thought-out and organized campaign. And if we succeed in Texas, we can succeed in any red state."

Harrison drummed his fingers on the table for several moments before saying, "That makes sense, but before I give the go-ahead, I'll need to see a cohesive plan."

Lawson frowned. "Come on, John, I thought I was done planning."

Harrison nodded. "Not really. You can't just light a fuse and walk away. So as soon as you get back to us with a detailed plan for flipping Texas, we'll turn you loose. But first things first—get to Thurston as soon as possible. Now then, I think that wraps things up for now. Meeting adjourned."

CHAPTER 7

▼

The Next Morning—CIA Headquarters, Langley, Virginia

After Lawson was seated and Martin's door closed, Lawson said, "Thanks, Phil, I hope I'm not taking you away from anything important."

Martin smiled. "It's business as usual, but for the moment implementing your plan is my number one priority. I agree with your plan of action for pursuing the revolution and will do all I can to help. Now then, our mystery author, now known as John Barlow, is expecting you for lunch at noon. That will give the two of you a little time to get reacquainted. Afterward you'll have until 1600 to conduct your business. When you're back we'll do a quick debriefing. Is that suitable?"

"Of course, Phil, and I appreciate your support on this project. Now where do I pick up my ride?"

Martin hit his intercom and said, "Please send Townsend in."

A moment later the door opened and a conservatively dressed man in his mid-thirties came into the office. Martin made the introduction. "Terry, this is Agent Townson, he'll be your escort today."

Lawson smiled, shook hands with Townson and said, "I didn't realize I would need an escort."

Martin smiled. "Townson is one of my best agents, and his current job is to ensure Barlow's security and function as our primary liaison with him."

Townson nodded and said, "And I like my job. Mr. Barlow is an excellent chess player and a damn good storyteller. So if you're ready, Mr. Lawson, you can follow me and I'll take you to our car."

Lawson turned to Martin before saying, "Thanks again, Phil. See you later."

As they walked down the corridor, Lawson said, "Do you have a first name, Agent Townson?"

"Yes, sir. It's Fred."

"Thank you, Fred. And I'm Terry."

Without changing his facial expression, Townson said, "Here we are. This elevator will take us to the lower level. Our car is waiting there at a side entrance."

The car proved to be an impressive black Cadillac Escalade with dark-tinted windows. After Lawson was seated behind the driver, Townson climbed into the front passenger seat. After nodding for the driver to go, Townson looked over his left shoulder and said, "The trip will take between forty and fifty minutes, depending on traffic."

"That's fine," Lawson said. "I brought lots of reading material and I enjoy sightseeing."

Lawson began his sightseeing as soon as the Escalade entered the GW Parkway and headed east along the Potomac River. After fifteen minutes of negotiating the streets of Northeast Washington, the SUV joined Route 50 East and began making its way into the verdant Maryland countryside. It was a bright sunny day, which enticed Lawson to frequently take in the picturesque scenery. Then, as they crossed over the Severn River, he looked to the right for a glimpse of the Naval Academy at Annapolis. Minutes later he again looked out as they began the three-mile crossing of the Chesapeake Bay Bridge. He was pleased to see that the sunny day had attracted dozens of sailboats that were tacking back and forth on the placid bay waters. It was a pleasant reminder of the many times he had done it himself.

When the Escalade pulled into the driveway of Barlow's safe house, Lawson looked at his watch—the trip had taken forty-five minutes. As soon as the vehicle stopped, Townson jumped out, opened the door for Lawson, and said, "Do you remember this place?"

Lawson smiled and nodded. "Only vaguely, but I do remember how secluded it was."

"Yes, sir, and as you can see, the trees and shrubs are maturing nicely. Mr. Barlow knows we're here, so we can go right in." Townsend bounded up the two steps to the small porch and entered a cipher code in the security box. When the lock clicked, he held the door open for Lawson to enter. As soon as Lawson was inside, he was greeted by Thurston, who said, "It's been a long time, Mr. Gray, and it's great to see you."

Lawson smiled. "And it's great to see you too, Sidney."

Thurston returned the smile and said, "I haven't heard that name in quite a while. I'm John Barlow now, living the good life and writing political commentary every now and then."

Lawson nodded. "I'm glad to see you're not overly busy, because I have a writing job for you."

Barlow smiled. "That's good, because I'm more than ready to knock out another book. What did you have in mind?"

"It'll take a little time to explain, so let's defer that until after lunch."

Barlow nodded. "That's fine. Now as for lunch, would you like to start with a little wine?"

Lawson smiled. "I never turn down an offer of wine, so that's a yes."

"Do you have a preference?"

"I'm partial to reds."

Thurston smiled. "Would a seven-year-old Vosne-Romanée be suitable?"

"Of course, it's one of my favorites."

"Mine also. That's why I picked up a few bottles while I was in Beaune last year."

Lawson laughed. "I envy you that experience. In my opinion the two best varietals in the world are the Pinot Noir and Chardonnay grapes grown in that region of Burgundy."

It was more than an hour later that Lawson and Barlow finished lunch and found their way to the den. Lawson initiated the conversation. "I'm sure you're aware that we patriots were only partially successful in cleaning up our government. Of course your book helped us immeasurably in dislodging Big Oil-sponsored Republicans from the White House. But it's unfortunate we weren't paying attention in 2010 and allowed the Tea Party to gain control of the House of Representatives. And to compound the problem, we failed to oust them in 2012. So once again our democracy is being threatened."

Barlow interrupted. "I'm well aware of what's going on. For the past several months my investigative juices have been flowing nonstop. So I'm primed to do some aggressive writing."

Lawson raised his eyebrows and said, "That's good to hear. Do you have anything particular in mind?"

Barlow nodded. "Yes, I do."

"Please share."

"As Sidney Thurston, investigative reporter, I wrote an exposé of Big Oil's hold on our government, which pissed off a lot of powerful people who put out a contract on me. Now, after two attempts on my life, I'm more than a little bitter and want revenge. So to answer your question, what I have in mind is writing a fictional autobiography of an investigative reporter named Christian Malloy."

Lawson laughed. "I like it. So, Christian, what's your *modus operandi?*"

"My primary objective is to rip the rich and powerful a new one while exposing the pervasive corruption of the Republican Party. Since I have the luxury of remaining anonymous, I can recklessly expose and attack without risk of reprisal. I can say, for instance, that every damn Republican in Congress is guilty of catering to the rich and powerful while completely neglecting the middle and working classes. And another luxury is having confidential informants to provide me with the information I need. Rather neat, wouldn't you say?"

Lawson smiled. "Damn neat. And your story will have authenticity because Sidney Thurston is known as a best-selling author."

"But one that's untouchable since he no longer exists."

Lawson smiled again. "I love the opportunity this presents. We patriots realize that we're not going to save democracy without informing the general public of what's really going on in Washington. We also realize that the only effective way to inform the public is via a smash movie. And a prerequisite for such a movie is a compelling story. Now then, that's where you come in, Sidney, a.k.a. Christian

Malloy. Do you have a compelling story to tell that's revelatory and entertaining?"

Thurston nodded. "I believe I do. For the past few months I've been doing research, mostly via the Internet, and have learned a lot. It's amazing that virtually everything one needs to know is available on the Internet. It's just a matter of finding it. I now know, for example, most of the details of President Kennedy's assassination—it was a very complex conspiracy. I also know that Big Oil's stranglehold on the government is greater than ever. The pervasive corruption of the Republican Party is quite remarkable. So, yes, I have a story to tell, and I'm ready to tell it. But I'll need a little help from my friends."

"What kind of help do you need?"

"The same kind of help I was given when I wrote my previous book. To make the story interesting as well as informative, I'll need details on the criminal and sexual transgressions of the prominent players in Washington."

Lawson nodded. "That should be no problem. Just let us know who in particular you want information on and we'll get it for you."

"You can start with the hypocritical Republican leadership, which includes the speaker of the House and the House majority leader. Those lying bastards need to be exposed."

"I must confess, Sidney, I think this project has great potential, so you'll get whatever you need from us."

"That's good, but I shouldn't need all that much. As I said, I've found a lot of interesting information on the Internet. For instance, when I was researching the Kennedy assassination, I came across a book that's extremely interesting. The title alone is dynamite."

"What's the book, Sidney?"

"The title is *Blood, Money, & Power: How LBJ Killed JFK*. It was written by an Austin attorney named Barr McClellan. It's an exceptionally well-written and exquisitely documented recounting of how, in 1962, the senior partner in his Austin law firm, a man named Edward Clark, received a total of eight million dollars from Clint Murchison Sr. to plan and carry out the assassination of John F. Kennedy. At the time Murchison was the wealthiest oil man in Texas and one of the wealthiest in the country. But in addition to his oil interests, Murchison was heavily invested in the military-industrial complex, which explains why he needed Johnson in the White House to initiate the Vietnam War."

Lawson shook his head. "I've been a longtime student of the Kennedy assassination and know most of the details, but it sounds like Mr. McClellan can fill in some gaps for me. What was your main take away from the book?"

"It just reinforces what we already knew about Big Oil's power and control over our governmental processes. But I did learn something that's germane to what's going on today."

"Which is . . . ?"

"That in 1948 Clint Murchison wanted his political puppet, Lyndon Johnson, in the Senate to position him for an eventual shot at the White House. So he paid Ed Clark to ensure that Johnson won the Democratic nomination, and at that time winning the nomination was tantamount to winning the election. Now in the first round of the Democratic primary the favored incumbent narrowly missed getting a majority of the votes. Johnson was a distant second. But amazingly, in the runoff, Johnson squeaked out a narrow 206-vote majority. Now how could that have happened? Well, the answer is that Clark, with Murchison's money, bought enough election officials to fix the outcome. But it wasn't easy. There were protests that were settled in various ways. Those that went to court were dismissed by paid-off judges. Those occurring in West Texas were settled when the protesting sheriffs committed suicide by shooting themselves in the back."

Lawson nodded. "How do you intend to use this information?"

Thurston smiled. "I'll get to that in a minute. Now here's what I think is really interesting about this bit of history. Fast forward to May 2012 in Texas. It's the first round of voting in the Republican primary for senator. The man you refer to as Mayhem finished second well behind a well-liked and respected member of the Texas government. The favored veteran won 44.6 percent of the votes while Mayhem trailed with only 34.2 percent. But in the runoff election, Mayhem gets 56.8 percent while his favored opponent gets just 43.2 percent. Isn't it interesting how similar that primary was to the one in 1948?"

Lawson nodded. "It's a replay—déjà vu. So Mayhem was boosted into the Senate the same way and for the same reason Johnson was. And again by Big Oil. Incredible."

"Isn't it? But before I can wrap up the story, I'll need to find out who put up the money for Mayhem and how they managed the turnaround."

Lawson nodded. "We'll do some digging and get you the answer. And when you lay out your book, don't forget that the theme is 'America can no longer afford the Big Oil-corrupted Republican Party.'"

"No problem, that's consistent with what I intended. All I need now are a few facts."

Lawson nodded. "We'll get you whatever you need. In return we expect a story that'll be compelling enough for Hollywood producers to fight for the rights to it."

Thurston smiled. "I expect the book will be every bit as compelling as the juicy stuff you feed me."

Lawson smiled and said, "Nice job, Sidney. You put the ball back in my court and that's fine. I'll be with you every step of the way on this project. And to wrap up, let me remind you we have to start making arrangements for publication as soon as possible. So the question is, how long will it take you to produce a publishable manuscript?"

"If I get in eight hours of writing every day, I can have a first-cut manuscript in four to five weeks. But for planning purposes allow another ten days to whip it into publication form."

"That sounds good. So whenever you have ad hoc information requirements, just pass them along to us via Townsend. And don't worry about progress reports, we'll be kept informed on how you're doing."

Thurston nodded and, as Lawson was leaving, shook his hand and said, "Thanks for putting me back to work . . . at something I love to do."

Lawson nodded. "You're welcome, and I'll expect to see you again in four or five weeks to review the manuscript. Good luck, Christian."

Back at Langley, the debriefing with Martin took only five minutes. After hearing Lawson's report, Martin suggested he return the next morning so they could include Hanley in a more detailed debriefing, especially regarding Thurston's information requirements.

CHAPTER 8

▼

The Next Morning, CIA Headquarters, Langley, Virginia

As soon as Lawson and Martin were seated in his office, Hanley pressed the intercom and told his secretary to hold all calls. After turning to Lawson, he said, "I understand your meeting with Thurston went pretty well. So what's the status of that effort?"

"Thurston is off and running with the book and expects to have a rough manuscript in thirty to forty-five days. That means we need to start making arrangements for publication as soon as possible. Phil, do you still control the publishing house we used for Thurston's previous book?"

Martin nodded. "The company's name is Burns and Solomon, and yes, we still have a controlling interest."

"Good. Can you alert them that in about forty days they'll be getting a manuscript for a new Thurston book?"

Martin smiled. "Certainly, and they'll be glad to hear that—they made a bundle from the last one."

Lawson nodded. "Also inform them that they'll only need to do the technical editing, that the content editing will have been done before they receive the manuscript. And since it's a follow-on, it should be blocked the same as the previous book."

Martin smiled. "I'm sure they'll know what you're talking about. But if they have any questions, I'll get back to you."

"Thanks, Phil," Lawson said before handing Hanley a sheet of paper and saying, "Jack, here are Thurston's current information requirements, which we can go over later. But while I've got you two together I'd like to discuss the most immediate and comprehensive of our pending ops—taking back Texas."

Hanley nodded, but Martin shook his head and said, "Please understand, Terry, I won't be contributing much to that operation. As you probably know, I've got a lot on my plate right now. My assets in the Middle East are working 24-7 to keep the region from blowing up. So I'm up to my ass in alligators, and it doesn't look like that's going to change anytime soon. To further complicate my life, we now have a major security problem running loose in Hong Kong. I'm sure you know that two days ago an NSA IT contractor turned up there, disclosing everything he knew about NSA's intelligence-gathering systems and processes. I expect the Chinese are already chatting with him."

Lawson frowned. "You're going to take him out, aren't you?"

Martin frowned. "That was the obvious move. But when I proposed it, our anal-retentive DCI got all political and contacted both the state department and the attorney general to get their blessings."

"And . . . ?"

"State is fearful of our diplomatic relations with China, and the attorney general doesn't want any action until he can figure out what to charge the asshole with."

Lawson looked astounded. "Good god, this is unbelievable. It's pretty damn obvious what he's guilty of—he's a traitor who's compromising our national security big-time."

"Of course, but that doesn't matter. Regardless of what we do, congressional Republicans are going to bellyache and the media will get all weepy about the son of a bitch's constitutional rights. Even more galling is the fact that he's revealing national secrets and compromising homeland security under the guise of being a whistle-blower—a whistle-blower who's informing the American public that their rights to privacy are being violated. I wonder if it ever occurred to clowns like him that the only people crying for privacy are those who are either doing something illegal or something they're ashamed of. And I'm sure that 90 percent of the people in this country care a hell of a lot more about being safe than they do about petty privacy."

Lawson frowned. "That's true. But this situation is just another example of why we have to put our revolution in high gear. Phil, it's understandable that your involvement will necessarily be limited. However, I believe Jack and I can handle most of what needs to be done in taking back Texas. Is that true, Jack?"

Hanley nodded. "I expect so. But don't forget, before we work on Texas, we've got to satisfy Thurston's information requirements."

When Martin heard that, he stood up and said, "I believe that's my exit cue. I'll leave you two to take care of Thurston," and he left.

Lawson nodded as Martin went out the door. He then turned to Hanley and said, "You're right, Thurston is our number one priority. And it's encouraging that he has a great idea on how to tell the story in his new book. He's going to write it from the perspective of a fugitive investigative reporter who reveals how the rich and powerful have co-opted the Republican Party and Congress. Of course in the process he'll continue nipping at Big Oil's ass. So to get started he needs revelatory information, salacious and otherwise, on the corruptors and their political prostitutes. Most immediately he wants to know which of the Big Oil guys is paying for Mayhem's drive to the White House. He needs that information to illustrate the eerie parallel between Johnson's path to the Senate in 1948 and how Mayhem was boosted into the Senate last year. Do you think you can handle that, Jack?"

Hanley nodded. "I'm sure we can, but it might take a little time."

"The sooner the better since Thurston wants to have a completed manuscript in thirty to forty days."

"Understood. What else does he need?"

Lawson nodded. "He wants as much personal dirt as he can get on both the Big Oil guys and the key Republicans in their pocket. Simply put, he'd like to know as much as possible about the sex lives of the rich and elected."

Hanley nodded. "Let me start by saying we can get most of what Thurston needs using standard counterintelligence techniques—spy-craft if you will. We can clone mobile devices, including smartphones, co-opt laptops, tap landlines, and install surveillance devices in our targets' homes and offices. We can track their movements and record most, but unfortunately not all their activities. What we can't routinely capture, for instance, is the ad hoc liaison of a congressman with a mistress or call girl. However, we found ways to cover those situations."

Lawson nodded. "By doing what?"

"The most basic way is by bugging the houses of mistresses, or the houses of congressmen who live alone and use their place for illicit sex. Another circumstance we now have covered is when a target routinely rents a hotel room for a noontime quickie. For example, if we hear a target make a noontime reservation at the Key Bridge Marriot, we know he'll be put in one of two rooms we have bugged. The arrangement costs us a few bucks, but it's well worth it. Another gap we now have covered is the situation in which a target randomly uses a high-class call girl and meets her in an ad hoc location. For that situation we've co-opted an upscale and discreet escort service that operates in DC. The operator of that service will give us advance notice of when and where a high-value target arranges to have sex with one of her girls. That advanced notification enables us to install surveillance devices at the liaison site and record all the action."

Lawson smiled. "That's impressive, Jack. You should be able to give Thurston exactly what he needs. It should also give us some interesting footage of our congressmen at work. We could post the most entertaining of those sessions on YouTube, which should create a serious media buzz."

Hanley held up his hand and said, "Interesting possibility, Terry, but hold on to that thought. For the time being we need to stay focused on Thurston's requirements. And I see from your list that he would like compromising information on the Republican leadership including the speaker of the House and the House majority leader."

Lawson nodded. "That's correct, and the remaining names are in priority order starting with the junior senator from Texas. He wants everything you can get on him, including his background, finances, tax information, his recreational preferences, and whatever else you think might be interesting."

Hanley nodded. "We can handle that."

"Good. Now the rest of the names on the list are my requirements, not Thurston's. They're the congressional Democratic leadership—the people we may need to blackmail into putting out the word on how congressional campaigns should be run. The remaining names are the Tea Party members from Texas. But I won't need that intelligence until our operation to turn Texas blue is launched."

Hanley nodded. "Got it, and for your information, I intend to use an off-campus control center in Rockville for these operations. If you remember, that's the one with a computer repair shop in the front and several control stations in the back."

Lawson nodded. "Yeah, and as I recall, you had a couple vans there that you used for work in the district.'

"That's right, and we still do. We have two three-man bugging teams that use the vans. As soon as we get an address where a target is having sex, a team is dispatched to bug the place. Two technicians go in and do the bugging while the third remains in the van as a lookout. If there's any danger, the lookout alerts the other two and, if necessary, physically intercepts the intruder."

"Thanks, Jack. I'm glad to see you have everything covered and that Thurston will get what he needs. Now with that said, there are a couple of other issues I'd like you to begin thinking about."

"Fine, what are they?"

"First on my list is gun violence and the NRA's role in subsidizing it. I'm totally pissed that the president of the NRA, in the wake of a mass shooting at the Newtown elementary school in Connecticut, is allowed by the major networks to claim that it never would have happened if the school had been secured and the teachers equipped with guns. What a crock. The facts are that the school was locked down and that the shooter got in by using his automatic weapon to shoot out a window. That lying son of a bitch went on to say that gun controls and a ban on automatic weapons wouldn't have prevented the tragedy. He then exploited his free airtime to spew more lies, such as saying that the president was about to take guns away from responsible gun owners. As you might guess, I despise the bastard."

Hanley nodded. "I think we all do, so how would you like me to handle it?"

"There are two problems to be solved. The first is that the president of the NRA is shilling for US gun manufacturers who only care about selling as many weapons as possible. He funnels their money through professional lobbyists to congressmen and state legislators who, in turn, block any attempt to pass restrictive gun laws. The second problem is that the conservative media covers up this corruption while providing a forum for progun spokesmen who spew an uninterrupted stream of bullshit. Those problems need to be addressed concurrently."

Hanley looked pensive for a few moments before saying, "Are there any rules of engagement for this operation?"

"No, do whatever it takes. However, I have two approaches in mind. The first is that the president of the NRA needs to be persuaded that continuing to corrupt government officials and heap blatant lies on the American people could be deleterious to his health. My second idea is to bypass the conservative media and communicate the truth about guns directly to the general public. Remember, two-thirds of today's voters own and use portable electronic communications devices, and easily half of them, especially younger voters, use one or more of the social media. In addition, most of them check out YouTube on a regular basis."

Hanley held up his hand and said, "I fully understand all that. What I don't know is how we leverage that fact."

Lawson smiled. "You'd make a good straight man, Jack. We leverage it by posting entertaining and informative video clips on YouTube. Early viewers of the clip can be expected to spread the word via Twitter, and before long a few million voters will have seen it. And of those millions, thousands will make tweets about it and/or copy it into their social network, and in that way, the word will spread exponentially."

Hanley nodded. "The video just has to be entertaining and informative, right?"

"Yes. Want an example?"

"That would be nice."

"Okay, here's the setup. The president of the NRA appears on the CBS evening news shortly after the mass killing of twenty grade school children and six adults by a deranged young man with an automatic weapon. He is allowed to speak without interruption. Rather than expressing condolences to the parents and the community, he defends the rights of the shooter to own and use an automatic weapon and blames society for the tragedy."

Hanley shook his head. "We know all that, so where are you going with it?"

Lawson smiled. "Be patient. While he's appearing on CBS, your people make a digital recording of his fatuous diatribe. The file is then passed to your creative video graphics people. They'll touch it up a bit and do a voice-over that has him saying something like, 'Can you believe that in light of that terrible tragedy in Connecticut, CBS is giving me this opportunity to feed you people a bunch of bullshit regarding guns? I'm exceptionally well paid to say ridiculous things like "Guns don't kill people, people kill people" and that the president is just looking for an excuse to take away your guns. But regardless of the fact that I'm paid a few million bucks a year to keep you people ignorant, I just can't do it any longer. The truth is that guns have only one purpose, and that's to kill things. Similarly the only purpose of automatic weapons is to kill multiple people in a matter of seconds. Given that, no one in the world should have an automatic weapon except trained military personnel. Look folks, it's way past time for my stooges in Congress to pass common-sense gun control laws. It's also way past time for the Second Amendment to be updated to reflect a modern-day definition of arms. Now, if you'll excuse me, I have to go and look for a new job.'"

Hanley laughed. "Want a little work as a scriptwriter, Terry?"

Lawson shook his head. "No thanks, Jack, I'm a bit busy right now. Besides, you already have people a lot more talented than me. But if you're shorthanded, think about acquiring one of those high-tech dot-com ad agencies. They're doing some really creative graphics work."

Hanley smiled. "Not to worry, Terry. Both Phil and I have highly talented graphics people who can produce anything you describe. Just let us know what you want."

"Thanks," Lawson said. "Now I'll let you get back to work. But I want to leave you with this thought—the constitution only says Americans have the right to bear arms, it says nothing about ammunition. With that reminder, I'll say adieu. Let me know when you have something for Thurston."

CHAPTER 9

▼

Later That Week at the Harrisons' House

When everyone was seated, Harrison said, "Before Terry explains his plan for taking back Texas, Jack has some relevant intelligence on its junior senator. Go ahead, Jack."

Hanley nodded and said, "This guy's an interesting piece of work. He was born in Canada while his parents were working there in the oil business. It's ironic, therefore, that while living in Canada, he and his parents were the beneficiaries of socialized medicine, of which he is now an outspoken opponent. He has a law degree and for a time served in the Texas government. He's married to an executive in a leading Wall Street firm who's making big bucks. And both of them had close ties to W's administration."

"Interesting," Lawson said. "So he's directly linked to both Big Oil and big Washington corruption. By the way, Jack, have you been able to determine which of the oil guys paid for his ride to the Senate?"

Hanley shook his head. "We think it was the Koch brothers but haven't been able to confirm it yet. We do know, however, that someone put up a lot of bucks for his senatorial campaign of which he's only spent a portion. That means he has a lot of money to work with in Washington. It's also interesting that since he took office, his net worth has swollen by more than a million. Based on our phone taps and a few excursions into his secured e-mail accounts, we have a good idea of where both the money and his marching orders are coming from. We know he was hired specifically to lead the Tea Party in its efforts to bring down the government. I believe that makes him the chief political terrorist in Congress and, as such, is an immediate threat to our democracy. He needs to be neutralized."

Martin raised a finger and said, "I'd be happy to take care of that."

Lawson shook his head. "He needs to go, Phil, but not that way. He's just a political prostitute doing what he's paid to do. Besides, we're going to make him the poster boy for everything that's wrong with the Republican Party these days. We'll identify him as the Republican leader of those opposing immigration reform, common-sense gun controls, and affordable health care for everyone. We can also highlight his role in getting legislation passed that discriminates against women and working-class minorities. And it'll be easy to demonstrate that he cares nothing about the people of Texas. Let the jerk explain why he's railing against the Affordable Care Act when 25 percent of his constituents have no health care insurance of any kind. Let him also explain his indifference to the plight of more than five million Texans who are living below the poverty level. That's a disgusting fact for a state that has forty-four billionaires. I expect Mayhem's perverted politics will be a wake-up call for both Texas and the nation. When we're done with him, I suspect even Republicans will want him to disappear."

Harrison smiled. "Go get 'em, Terry. Now let's hear the rest of your plan for Texas."

Lawson nodded. "I'll start by reiterating what I said at the last meeting that there's an urgency for initiating the next phase of our revolution in Texas. And that's because Big Oil, fronted by the Republican Party, owns and operates the state in a fashion that's detrimental to the entire country. So if we expect to have any real success nationally, we have to take on Big Oil and free up the Lone Star state. With that said, I believe our objective and slogan for this op should be 'Take Back Texas,' and the code name for the operation should simply be the initials TBT. Any comments so far?"

Harrison nodded. "That works for me. I like both the concept and the cryptic code name. Does anyone else have a question or comment?"

Martin raised a finger. "In this op, is our primary target Big Oil or the Republican Party?"

"Actually both," Lawson said, "because we'll need to deal with the money of Big Oil as well as the Texas Republican politicians they own."

Martin nodded. "Will we need to terminate any of the Big Oil guys this time around?"

Lawson shook his head. "I don't anticipate that being necessary. I expect we can accomplish our mission simply by making a few of them less wealthy and less relevant. Are there any other questions?"

Heads shook so Lawson continued, "Now then, the principal objective of operation TBT is to enable Texas Democrats to win the governor's mansion, a majority in the legislature, and a majority of its congressional seats. And that includes the one now occupied by its senior senator. I believe all that can be accomplished with two initiatives. The first would be to provide guidance to the Democratic organizations on how to indoctrinate their candidates to run winning campaigns, and on how to conduct effective get-out-the-vote operations at election time. The second initiative would be to provide financial assistance to key campaigns."

Harrison raised a finger. "When you say 'financial assistance,' do you mean assisting Democratic organizations to raise money, or by our contributing money directly to their campaigns?"

Lawson nodded. "Probably both. To figure out how much we might have to contribute, we'll need intelligence on the amount the conservative big boys will be kicking in for their candidates. We'll also need to determine how much Democrats can expect to raise on their own. I suspect there'll be a deficit, so we should be prepared to put up the difference."

Harrison raised his eyebrows and said, "Phil has informed me that we could probably donate around thirty million and possibly as much as fifty million. But if we did fifty million, it would exhaust our cash resources, leaving nothing for the national campaigns. So we need to think this through."

Jennifer raised a finger. "John is right. To win nationally, progressives will need substantially more money than we can provide. And there's no question that the titans that traditionally finance the Republican Party will be putting up a bundle in an attempt to save their sorry asses. So here's my thinking. We need to find our own titans—ultra wealthy people who really give a damn about this country and are willing to invest in saving it."

Harrison smiled. "Good thinking, my dear, I believe you hit the nail on the head. Now how do we find these titanic patriots?"

Lawson nodded. "I have an idea on how to start. I came here tonight to propose that Lan and I initiate Operation TBT by going to Texas for a firsthand look at the political landscape there. And Jennifer has given us a reason to go as soon as possible: Keep in mind, Texas has forty-four billionaires and not all of them are cozy with Big Oil. As a consequence I think it's likely there are at least a couple who would like to see Texas wrenched away from Big Oil and would invest in making that happen. The payback for them would be that the state's middle and working classes would become better educated, have more purchasing power, and thus give the Texas economy a significant boost, which would benefit everyone. So by going down there soonest and establishing some connections, Lan and I might be able to identify one or more of these patriots."

"I think that's a good idea," Harrison said. "So when do you want to go?"

Lawson nodded. "I'm ready to go now, and I suspect Lan is as well."

When Lawson looked at her, she nodded.

Seeing this, Harrison said, "What's your plan?"

"Well, the first thing we need to do is find a respected Democrat there with political savvy to front for us. He'll be the one to help determine the feasibility of what we're trying to so. And fortunately I know just the man. He's a highly respected eleven-term congressman who recently retired. As I understand it, he retired because he was totally frustrated by the obstructionist Tea Party clowns who are dedicated solely to bringing down the government. And he's a Hispanic with close ties to the administration. I'm relatively sure he'd jump at the chance to help us take back Texas and eradicate the Tea Party."

"Do you know this man?"

"Yes, but only slightly. When I was at Randolph Air Force Base in San Antonio in the seventies, I campaigned for his father. His father was a remarkable long-term congressman and civil rights activist.

When his father passed away, he won the seat and has served until now. I had the pleasure of meeting him one time at a social affair in San Antonio. That was about a year ago when I was visiting my daughter's family."

"Do you think he'd remember you?"

"Probably not, but I could remind him of that chance meeting."

Harrison nodded. "Can I assume you'll be visiting your daughter sometime soon?"

"I think Lan can answer that question."

She smiled and said, "Terry knows I always enjoy visiting the River Walk. We can be ready to go as soon as travel arrangements are made."

Jennifer nodded. "I'll take care of that. Do you have any preferences for a hotel?"

"The Hyatt Regency is always good. It's centrally located and just a couple blocks from the Palm Restaurant."

"Good. I should have your flight and hotel reservations no later than tomorrow. So plan to travel the day after."

Lan nodded. "We'll be ready."

Lawson smiled and said, "As usual Lan speaks for me. But before we depart I'll need the contact information for my man. His name is Charles Garcia."

Hanley nodded. "We'll have that and a full bio for you tomorrow."

"Thanks, Jack. In the meantime I'll develop a legend along the lines of being the representative of a small group of very wealthy people who are disgusted with the way Congress is behaving, especially the Texas contingent. I'll tell Garcia my friends have authorized me to contribute whatever amount of money is needed to take back Texas. How does that sound?"

Harrison nodded. "That should work. Of course, you have the flexibility to improvise based on Garcia's level of interest."

"Sure, I'll be prepared to do that. Oh, and don't forget to give me the mobile numbers you want us to use to contact you while we're there."

Jennifer nodded. "Everything you'll need will be included in your travel package."

Harrison slapped the table and said, "It seems we're about to fire the first shot in the second phase of our revolution. Everyone will be kept informed as needed, and we'll meet back here when Terry has something to report. So as Ed Murrow would say, 'Good night, and good luck.'"

CHAPTER 10

▼

Three Days Later, San Antonio, Texas

After giving the bellhop a five-dollar tip, Lawson turned to Lan and said, "It's nearly seven. Let's hit the bar for a drink and then navigate our way along the River Walk to Luciano's. I'm hungry for a little linguini with red clam sauce."

Lan nodded. "Let's go. We can unpack after dinner."

Lawson hesitated, looked pensive, and said, "I just had a thought. Since Garcia has an executive job with the city government, he'll probably be working tomorrow. So I should call him now."

Lan flicked her hand and said, "Go ahead. I'll find something in the minibar to tide me over."

Lawson checked his notebook, found Garcia's home phone number, and keyed it in on his mobile. When Garcia answered, Lawson said, "Good evening, Congressman, I hope I'm not disturbing you. My name is Terry Lawson. We met at a social function about a year ago and had a brief chat. You probably don't remember me, but at the time I told you I had lived in San Antonio in the seventies and did a bit of campaigning for your father."

"Yes, I remember," Garcia said. "You were in the air force then, weren't you?"

"That's right, sir. And when I retired from the air force, I settled in McLean, Virginia, where I had the opportunity to read the *Washington Post* daily. That's how I followed your remarkable career in Congress. Needless to say, I was very disappointed when I learned you were retiring. And that brings me to the reason I'm calling you. I'm staying at the Hyatt Regency for a couple days and was hoping we could meet for lunch, preferably tomorrow. Among other things I'd like to discuss your reason for retiring. I think you'll find the meeting worthwhile."

"You're invitation sounds intriguing, Mr. Lawson, a bit reminiscent of those furtive lunches I had in Washington."

Lawson chuckled. "I'm glad you mentioned lunches in Washington, sir. I expect you had a few at the Palm on Nineteenth Street. So for nostalgia's sake I'd like to meet you at the Palm here in San Antonio. As you probably know, it's on South Houston Street."

"That would be fine. What time did you have in mind?"

"Would twelve thirty work for you?"

"Indeed, so twelve thirty it is."

"Then I shall see you tomorrow. Good evening, sir."

Turning to Lan, Lawson said, "As you heard, the meeting is set."

"Good. Now I'd like you to buy me a drink."

After returning to their room from breakfast the following morning, Lawson did a fast scan of *USA Today*. Finding nothing of interest in the paper, he spent a few minutes reviewing Garcia's bio. When he put the paper aside, Lan said, "Do you want to rehearse?"

Lawson shook his head. "Not really, I think I'm good."

Lan smiled. "I admire your confidence. What did you do when you were living in McLean?"

"What do you mean 'what did I do'?"

"What did you do for a living?"

"You know damn well what I did for a living."

"Of course, but Garcia doesn't."

Lawson smiled. "You think I should rehearse, don't you?"

"It wouldn't hurt. So what did you do for a living while in McLean?"

"When I retired from the air force, I worked as a senior consultant for Booz Allen Hamilton. My primary clients were the Departments of Defense and Energy. Five years later, I became the director of systems development for the MCI Corporation. I was there when MCI took AT&T to court and won a 1.8-billion-dollar award.

After my stint at MCI, I formed my own corporation to do business at the highest levels of the Department of Defense. I succeeded in selling DoD a systems development technology I invented, which enabled them to develop functional systems twice as fast and for half the cost they were currently paying. That success enabled me to become rather wealthy which, in turn, enabled me to write political commentaries and op-ed pieces for the *Post*, decrying the governmental and social deterioration of this country."

Lan smiled. "A little long-winded and grandiose, but it should get his attention."

"Thank you, dear. Do you have any other questions?"

"Just one—what are you currently doing with your wealth?"

"As I said before, I'm collaborating with wealthy friends who want to rescue our nation from the radical right, which is undermining our democracy and destroying our country."

Lan laughed. "I hope Garcia is a keen and patient listener."

Lawson smiled. "Not to worry, I can tailor my responses to his apparent level of interest. Isn't that what you do when you're interviewing prospective agents?"

"Of course, but in this case there's a lot more at stake."

"I know, and from what I know about Garcia, he's a person that really gives a damn about people and this country. Like his father, he's always been a champion of minorities and the underprivileged. I like our chances with him."

"What now?"

"It's time for me to call the Palm and make a reservation."

Lawson arrived at the Palm Restaurant at 1220 and took a booth near the front entrance. He ordered a martini to sip on while he waited. Just before 1230, Charles Garcia came through the front door and was quickly ushered to Lawson's booth. Lawson stood up, shook hands with Garcia, and said, "Good to see you, sir. I hope this meeting isn't inconveniencing you."

Garcia smiled and said, "Not at all. I was looking forward to meeting you. And please call me Charlie."

Lawson returned the smile. "Charlie it is. And I'm Terry. Would you care for a drink?"

"Yes and no. Yes, I would like one, but no, I'm not having one. I have to stay relatively coherent for a business meeting this afternoon."

Lawson laughed. "I know what you mean. But since I'm fully retired, it's a luxury I now enjoy whenever I can."

At that moment the waiter, attired in black-tie, came to the table and said, "Can I get you gentlemen anything to drink?"

Garcia shook his head and said, "Just water."

The waiter turned to Lawson, who said, "Water for me also and a glass of Pinot Noir with the meal." Lawson then turned to Garcia and said, "Charlie, how about a glass of wine with your lunch? It's good for your digestion and helps clear your mind."

Garcia smiled and nodded. "That's true, so a glass of Pinot Noir for me as well."

The waiter made a note and said, "Shall I give you gentlemen a few more minutes to look over the menu?"

Lawson nodded. "Please, I'll let you know when we're ready." Lawson took a sip of his martini and said, "Am I right, Charlie, in thinking you retired from Congress because of the frustration and futility of trying to deal with those obstructionist Tea Party idiots?"

Garcia nodded. "That's the most significant reason. Another reason, however, is that I'd like to increase my income. My father once said, 'No one should leave Congress with more money than they went in with.' I was in debt then, and I'm still in debt."

Lawson laughed. "I fully understand. And I think—and hope— that the proposition I'm about to put forward will be of interest to you, for both those reasons."

Garcia smiled. "That's possible, but I have a job I enjoy and the pay is quite satisfactory."

"That's fine, because what I'm about to offer you would enable you to keep your current job."

Garcia looked quizzical and said, "You now have my full attention."

Lawson smiled. "Good, now by way of background, let me tell you who I represent. I represent a small group of wealthy patriots who are concerned about the tenuous state of our democracy. They believe, as I do, that ultra wealthy conservatives, fronted by the Republican Party, have corrupted Congress to the extent that nothing beneficial is getting done, especially for our middle and working classes."

Garcia nodded and said, "That's true. Please continue."

"As I was saying, my friends and I know the corruption currently paralyzing Washington has its roots in Texas. We're appalled that the previous Republican administration, Texans all, so callously devastated this nation—first by allowing 9/11 to happen, then by thrusting us into an unnecessary war that devastated a country and cost thousands of American lives and tens of thousands of Iraqi lives. To further compound their transgressions, that criminal administration ran up a five-trillion-dollar national debt, due in large part to the fact that their war of choice was unfunded, and to cap off their abysmal time in office, those Texans plunged the country into a deep recession. I realize you know all this, but I'm making the point that my friends are concerned that the Big Oil-funded politicians of Texas are again jeopardizing the welfare of this country."

Garcia nodded. "You're right, I'm well aware of what you've just told me, and I'm disgusted. So what do your people intend to do about this frustrating situation?"

"In a nutshell, we want to eradicate the corruption in Washington at its roots here in Texas. Our intention is to take back the state from the Republicans and thus sever Big Oil's stranglehold on both Texas politics and the federal government."

Garcia smiled. "I understand and applaud your intentions. And as you may or may not know, there's a nascent effort here in Texas to do just that—turn the state blue. You and your people might be well served to look into that effort."

Lawson looked surprised. "That's good to hear. How much do you know about the movement?"

"Very little," Garcia said. "And given that, I fail to see how I might help you."

"Quite the contrary," Lawson said. "By simply informing me of the movement, you already have. Look, Charlie, I wouldn't be talking to you if we didn't think you could be a significant help. You're still respected on Capitol Hill, and just as importantly, you're highly respected here in Texas. Since my friends and I are prepared to do whatever is required to take Texas back from the oil barons, we need someone with your credentials and creditability to front our effort. We want to remain in the background as much as possible."

Garcia smiled. "I'm flattered, but I still fail to see how I can help in more than a superficial way."

Lawson nodded. "First of all, we want your assessment of what it will take to rescue Texas from the Republicans."

Garcia smiled. "Let me start by saying I'm not sure it's feasible."

Lawson looked startled. "Why do you say that?"

"Mainly because in the last gubernatorial election, our infamous governor failed to win a single urban county, but he did win every rural county and the election. And I don't see that situation changing."

Lawson shook his head. "Not even with substantial financial support?"

"I'm afraid not. Let me explain the situation. Republicans have controlled those rural counties for so long now that their conservative candidates usually run unopposed. So there is no reason to expect rural voters to vote any differently than they have for years."

"Can't that be changed?"

Garcia shook his head. "I don't see how. But I am hearing a buzz that Democrats think they can make inroads in the rural counties around and south of San Antonio."

"Would an infusion of financial support for the Democratic committees in the rural counties help?"

Again Garcia shook his head. "No, because the fundamental problem is that in most rural counties, there's seldom a viable Democratic presence."

"That's depressing. Any suggestions on how we might proceed?"

"As I just mentioned, there's a latent belief that if enough southern counties are turned, we have a chance to win the gubernatorial election. But as always, that'll take a lot of sweat and money."

Lawson nodded. "If it's even remotely possible, we'll support the effort."

Garcia smiled. "Well, there's always hope, isn't there? If nothing else, the gubernatorial race will be interesting since a woman named Wendy Davis has already registered for the Democratic primary."

Lawson drew back his head. "I didn't think that was possible in Texas."

Garcia nodded. "Well, it's true, and she has at least as much chance of winning as a male would."

"That's good to hear. What do you like about her?"

"Well, to start with, she's a very intelligent state senator and an outspoken proponent of women's rights—something in short supply in Texas. Several weeks ago, she filibustered against a blatantly discriminatory piece of legislation by the all-white male Republicans. She did it nonstop for more than thirteen hours until the legislative session ended. She got national attention for doing so. Plus she's a self-made woman who pulled herself up by her bootstraps. She was raised by a single mother in poor circumstances and found herself a single mother when she was only twenty. But she worked hard, managed to attend TCU, and finished first in her class. After that she graduated from Harvard Law with honors. She's a shining example of someone living the American dream."

Lawson nodded. "That's a very impressive story. I read about her filibuster in the *Washington Post*, and the article was accompanied by a picture—a rather attractive lady."

"That's true, and another impressive thing about her is that she's an accomplished public speaker. She'll do well in debates."

Lawson shook his head. "Shame on you, Charlie, you had me thinking I was here on a fool's errand. With a torchbearer like her, I would say there's a damn good chance."

Garcia smiled. "Don't forget, Terry, you're still in Texas. The politics here are rough-and-tumble and generally not too hospitable for women."

"And that's why I'm here. That situation has to change, and it can with help from someone like you. My friends and I have the resources to facilitate that change, but we need to be pointed in the right direction. If you provide the know-how and guidance needed, we'll make it happen. And we'll compensate you generously for your help."

Garcia smiled. "I'm flattered by what you say. However, I'm uncertain whether I could handle what you're expecting of me in addition to my current job."

Lawson nodded. "We can make it relatively easy for you to handle both, and here's how. We'll immediately put you on retainer to serve as our legal counsel in Texas. In that capacity you would represent us whenever needed. For example, if you think it constructive for us to support the movement to turn Texas blue, you would serve as the interface for us doing so. And we'll provide whatever legal assistance you might need to accomplish that."

Garcia shook his head. "Again, your offer is very attractive, and I would be lying if I said I wasn't interested. But this is a matter I need to discuss with my family. I'm sure you can understand they come first in my life. Can I have until tomorrow noon to give you an answer?"

"That would be fine. Now then, are you ready to eat?"

Garcia smiled. "I'm more than ready. I had no idea discussing a revolution could give one such an appetite."

Lawson smiled and nodded to the waiter.

CHAPTER 11

▼

The Following Day

Lawson clicked a number on his iPhone and waited a few moments before saying, "Garcia is on board. To seal the deal I promised him a ten-thousand-dollar retainer, so please ask Mr. Black to wire that amount as soon as practical. I'll e-mail you his bank's routing number and his account number."

Lawson listened for several more seconds before saying, "No, he's the real deal. He didn't take the job for the money. He's still frustrated at how Republicans in general and the Tea Party in particular have been debilitating the federal government. He disliked them when he was a member of Congress and he detests them even more now. I think Charlie—that's what he asked to be called—is highly motivated to have Congress cleaned up. Oh, and he's already started earning his retainer. He told me about an emerging Democratic effort to turn Texas blue. From what I was told, it has the same purpose as our TBT operation."

After listening for a bit, Lawson said, "Lan and I will be arriving National at 2110. We should be home around 2200. I'll check in with you then to provide more details."

Lan, who was sitting on the edge of the bed, said, "Was he pleased?"

"It's hard to tell with John. But he did use the word *good* once."

Lan smiled. "I know. But he should have said that he was pleased that you accomplished what you did."

Lawson shook his head. "Actually it fell a bit short of what John and the rest of us expected. Operation TBT is going to be more difficult than we anticipated."

Lan frowned and said, "Well, I think you did an excellent job, both yesterday and last night."

Lawson laughed. "Thank you, dear. Now how about a pitcher of sangria and a little Mexican for lunch? Afterward we'll do what the locals do."

"And what would that be?"

"Go into seclusion for a little siesta."

Lan cocked her head, squinted, and said, "Is siesta a time for resting or reproduction?"

"It can be for both. We start with a Mexican lunch along the River Walk. The sun beaming down on us is pleasant and warm, so we're forced to drink a great deal of cool and refreshing sangria. By the end of the meal, the sun has warmed our bodies from head to toe and the sangria has warned our innards. The desire to make love overcomes us, so we hurry back to the hotel. Then, after a protracted lovemaking session, we lie back for a refreshing nap."

"Will the first phase of this siesta require another thirty-two-dollar pill?"

"Not if we have enough sangria."

"In that case let's go find some sangria."

The flight from San Antonio to Washington's Reagan National Airport was relatively uneventful, arriving five minutes early—a notable accomplishment for United. Fifteen minutes later, after claiming their baggage, the Lawsons grabbed a cab to take them to their house in McLean. On the cab ride home, Lawson called the Harrisons. When his call was answered, Lawson listened carefully and then frowned. He looked at Lan and shook his head. A moment later he said, "Got it. See you then."

When Lan looked questioningly, Lawson said, "John has called an emergency meeting for tomorrow evening. Apparently the Tea Party assholes are up to their old tricks, but this time for exceptionally high stakes."

Lan frowned. "Any preparation required?"

"Nothing specific, John just said we'll be going to the mats."

"Good, I'm ready. It's way past time for us and the administration to go on the offensive. Those political terrorists have been getting away with far too much for far too long."

Lawson nodded, "Good, you're all fired up and ready to go. However, job one at the moment is to get a good night's sleep."

Lan smiled. "That should be no problem, even without a sleeping pill."

Lawson laughed. "I'm sure the one you got this afternoon will get you through the night."

Lan shook her head but didn't comment.

CHAPTER 12

▼

The Evening of the Following Day, at the Harrisons' House

When everyone was seated at the conference table, John said, "This emergency meeting was called because Jack's people have developed some critical intelligence. Jack."

Looking uncommonly serious, Hanley said, "We've tapped into a highly coordinated plan on the part of the Tea Party to shut down the government by stonewalling any budget agreement. They then plan to prevent Congress from raising the debt ceiling. The effect of those two subversive actions will effectively disable the government and throw the economy into chaos, undoubtedly damaging this country irreparably. This is an unqualified act of political terrorism and needs to be dealt with immediately."

Lawson raised a finger. "Have you discussed this with Phil?"

"Yes."

"And . . . ?"

"We're in accord that this conspiracy is an overt act of terrorism and needs to be nipped in the bud. The principal obstacle, as always, is that the conspiracy is apparently funded by the brothers Grimm who make no secret of the fact they want the government to fail. So make no mistake about it, these guys are big-time anarchists who have enough Tea Party congressmen by the short hair to make it happen."

Lawson frowned. "Looks like we're headed for a serious battle, so please allow me to characterize our targets."

Harrison nodded. "Go ahead, Terry."

"Thanks, John," Lawson said. "We've recognized from the beginning that the people hijacking our democracy are, for the most part, white Anglo-Saxon males. This bunch comprises the ultra wealthy, the CEOs of large corporations, and the leaders of special interest groups. A common quirk of these white supremacist males is that they surround themselves with people who look like them, dress like them, and think like them, which of course reveals their latent racism. And their common bond is that they're all card-carrying members of the elitist Republican Party."

Harrison interrupted. "Where are you going with this, Terry?"

"I'm about to make the point that the largely white male Republican Party has made no secret of its desire to have our biracial president fail. And they are doing everything in their power to make that happen. The Tea Party members, who come across as being brain-dead, are just foot soldiers in this ultra-conservative Republican crusade. And lest we forget, most of these Tea Party idiots are from the Deep South where their male antecedents dressed up in white sheets and hoods and murdered innocent blacks."

Harrison shook his head. "Well, that's dramatic, Terry, but I still don't see your point."

"The point I'm trying to make is that the Tea Party has no other objective than to bring down the government and the president with it. That makes them anarchists and, as such, should be dealt with severely."

Martin smiled. "Now you're talking my language, Terry. Let me know if you would like any of those rednecks eliminated."

Harrison rapped his knuckles on the table and said, "Hold on, Phil. You're forgetting what we learned in Vietnam, which was, 'if you want to kill the snake, you cut off its head.' Our successful hit on Osama bin Laden is the most recent example of that philosophy in practice."

Martin nodded. "You're right, John. So whose head should we take off?"

"It seems obvious to me the snake is a two-headed one—the brothers Grimm. Everything they've done in politics has been aimed at eliminating any government control over the private sector."

Lawson nodded. "That's right, John, but the probability of successfully taking them out is asymptotic to zero. So let's focus on their current champion, Senator Mayhem."

It was Hanley's turn to speak. "I agree, Terry. We have information that the brothers have already pipelined a substantial amount of money to him which he is supposed to share with his Tea Party colleagues. But as far as we can determine, he hasn't been doing that. Whether that's the case or not, we can inform his Tea Party buddies he's been skimming money due them."

Harrison shook his head. "I agree we should initiate action against the senator, but I also feel strongly that we should expose the brothers as the financial bullies and white-gloved anarchists they are."

Hanley raised a finger. "I think we have a good start in doing that. We know, for instance, the brothers were instrumental in getting that asinine Citizens United Supreme Court decision that declared corporations are people. Here's how they did it. In the weeks prior to that irrational decision, they wined and dined the two conservative justices who engineered the decision. We have dates, times, and details of those occasions."

"That's good, Jack," Harrison said. "But for the moment we need to focus our attention and resources on breaking up the stranglehold the Tea Party has on the House of Representatives."

Lawson nodded. "There's no question of that. So let's leave it to Thurston to do a comprehensive job on the brothers Grimm in his book. Now regarding this immediate situation, I have a question. Of the forty Tea Party members in the House, can you identify the leaders?"

Hanley nodded. "Yeah, we've already done that. There are ten who appear to dominate. Those ten are the ones who usually speak on the floor and/ or hold press conferences."

"Good," Lawson said. "I suggest we initially focus on those ten. Dredge up as much dirt as you can on them, and if any are relatively clean, fabricate something."

Hanley nodded. "We can do that. We already have the ten fully tapped, which includes their mobile phones as well as their office and home phones. We also have access to their iPads, laptops, and desktops. We'll record everything going in and out of those devices including text messages and e-mails. That should give us enough culpable information to start applying serious pressure."

Harrison nodded. "Sounds like a plan, Jack. The name of the operation will be Ice Breaker and Jack has the lead. Jennifer and I will coordinate. Terry, you, and Lan stand by to give Jack any additional help he needs in researching the backgrounds of the targets. That's it for now. Jennifer will notify you regarding our next meeting."

CHAPTER 13

▼

A Week Later—the Harrisons' House

When everyone was seated, John Harrison said, "Well, we're too late. Those Tea Party bastards have shut down the government, and it's negatively impacting most everyone in this country. Jack, are we prepared to make those morons realize the error of their ways?"

Hanley nodded and said, "We have enough on eight of the principals to tarnish their public image and piss off their constituents. They've been getting a significant amount of money under the table and stashing it in offshore accounts. That means they are, or will be, guilty of federal income tax evasion. Five are cheating on their wives, and we have videos of three of them in the act."

Harrison smiled. "So how do you recommend we proceed?"

Lawson raised a finger and said, "I think the first step is to make the targets aware of what we know about them and that our intention is to go public unless they reconsider their position on keeping the government shutdown, and/or not raising the debt ceiling. If that doesn't get their attention, we can drain a significant amount of the money from their offshore accounts and let them know the rest will be gone in a flash if they don't stop their obstructionism."

Harrison thought for a few moments before saying, "That should work. Jack, can you handle it?"

Hanley nodded. "Yes, of course. We can use both secured voice mails and e-mails to threaten them. We can also hack into their smartphones and computers to drop threatening messages. At minimum they'll see the extent to which we have them by the balls."

Harrison smiled. "Pressure them in every way possible. I want these clowns looking over their shoulders every minute of every day."

Lawson shook his head. "The only problem I see is that we won't know if we were successful until the next floor vote is taken. And that could be as long as ten days from now. In the meantime the shutdown is costing the public nearly two billion a day, more than enough to pay for the complete implementation of the Affordable Care Act. So there's no way in hell the Tea Party morons will be able to explain that to voters."

Jennifer nodded. "What we're getting out of all this is some impressive wasted dollar figures to use as a hammer in next year's congressional elections. The longer this shutdown goes on, the greater our dollar-based leverage will be. No congressman can get reelected if the voters in his or her congressional district realize the billions of dollars he or she helped squander."

Harrison smiled at his wife and said, "Very astute, dear. Of course, your reasoning suggests that the longer the government is shut down, the bigger the hammer we'll have in 2014."

Jennifer thought for a moment before saying, "That's essentially true, but the increase in leverage when the waste goes from five billion to ten billion is relatively small. For most people, a billion is hard to comprehend, let alone five or ten billion."

"Good point, Jennifer," Lawson said. "Let's make it easier for voters to understand the monetary impact of the shutdown by showing them that for every day the government is shut down, the cost to each man, woman, and child in this country is more than eighty dollars. For example, if the shutdown goes on for fifteen days, the cost to a family of four would be nearly five thousand dollars. Since many voters vote their pocketbook, that by itself should be enough to bury the Tea Party in 2014."

Hanley smiled. "I like what I'm hearing, so Operation Ice Breaker is now in effect. We'll start taking action first thing tomorrow."

Harrison nodded. "Good, Jack. As usual keep us informed of your progress. I want this operation to be clean and surgical—no fingerprints."

"That goes without saying," Hanley said with a smile.

CHAPTER 14

▼

The Following Day, CIA Headquarters, Langley, Virginia

Hanley looked at his watch as he walked down the corridor to his office. He was five minutes late, which meant he was about to hear from his prickly secretary, Janice. When he entered his office, she didn't disappoint. "Did we get a little extra shut-eye this morning, sir?" she said.

Hanley frowned. "Hardly, my driver was late picking me up."

Janice shook her head. "You never fail to disappoint me. As a career intelligence officer, you should be a much better liar. Your driver called and said you were running late. Want to try again?"

"No, and I trust you have my damn coffee ready."

"The only reason I come in so damn early is so your damn coffee will be ready whenever you damn well decide to get here. It'll be on your damn desk in fifteen seconds."

Hanley smiled and said, "Good morning, Janice. And yes, fifteen seconds will be fine. Now as much as I would like to continue bantering with you, I must forego doing so. I have a very busy day ahead of me."

After setting a coffee cup on Hanley's desk, Janice said, "Of course you do. Why should today be any different than any other day? Now be careful of the coffee, it's damn hot."

"Thank you, Janice. Remind me to give you a raise sometime next year. In the meantime, would you please ask Van Morton to come to my office and bring yesterday's transcripts with him?"

Janice did an abbreviated curtsy and said, "It shall be done, sir."

As she was leaving, Hanley said, "Please close the door behind you." As soon as the door closed, Hanley took off his jacket and hung it on the clothes tree behind his desk. After getting comfortable in his leather executive chair, he pulled a red folder from his briefcase and began scanning the contents.

Minutes later, Hanley heard via the intercom that Morton had arrived. Before he could say, "Send him in," the door opened and his technical assistant entered. "Good morning, sir," Morton said.

"Good morning, Van. Did you get any sleep last night?"

"Enough, I suppose. I think you'll be pleased with the progress we've making with the intel you requested."

"Do you have transcripts for me to look at, or are you going to brief me?"

"I do have transcripts, which I'll leave with you, but I'm prepared to brief you if you like."

"Yes, I like, but just the executive summary."

Morton nodded. "The bottom line on the ten we've been monitoring is that they all have the same marching orders, which is to reject any legislation that might be viewed as a plus for the president. It's clear that their mission is to ensure the president is viewed as a failure."

Hanley nodded. "Well, that confirms the obvious."

"It does indeed. But what's not so obvious is how they operate in lockstep."

"And how do they manage that?"

"Eight of the ten we're monitoring function as coordinators for the Tea Party caucus. Using smartphones, each of the eight informs four of their colleagues on where to meet, what to say, and how to vote."

Hanley smiled. "That's the same technique flash mob coordinators use, isn't it? So do you have the numbers of all the caucus members?"

Morton shook his head. "No, not all, but we do have the numbers of the leadership cadre. So we hear all the coordinating calls between the leadership and their minions. Now it's a bit surprising that they're not using any security software to screen their calls. So we can listen in whenever we want."

"Is that oversight a function of ignorance or arrogance?"

"I suspect a little of both. It appears many of these esteemed congressmen have red necks under their white collars."

Hanley chuckled. "It's wonderful to have naive targets for a change. Do you have any additional blackmail material on the elite eight?"

"We've recorded another one having sex with a call girl at the Washington Hilton. That gives us four, and we expect to record at least two more before we're done. It's interesting that none of the performances we've seen so far are in any way impressive."

Hanley chuckled. "So it appears they don't perform any better in bed than they do in Congress."

Morton laughed. "That's about it. Now here's a look ahead. The proprietor of our honey trap told us we could expect the house majority leader to call for an appointment at some point in the near future. She said he was overdue for a hookup."

Hanley slapped his desktop. "That's excellent. Let me know immediately if you record him in the act. He's a super hypocrite that should be castrated. Our in-house author, Sidney Thurston, would love to see some footage of him in the saddle. What else do you have on the Tea Party leadership?"

"In addition to their sexual indiscretions, we have illegal financial transactions along with chronic drug and alcohol use."

Hanley nodded. "So all of them can be blackmailed, right?"

"Yes, to varying degrees. But my thinking is that rather than initially going after them individually, we make a broad generic threat spelling out the consequences of obstructing much-needed legislation. We can tell them, for instance, that their repetitious attempts to withhold affordable health care from forty million Americans is totally repugnant and unacceptable. We can then apprise them that if anyone dies for lack of such affordable care, they will be collectively held responsible and dealt with accordingly. To give authenticity to our threat, we throw in the details of what we know about their individual indiscretions. That should make clear the extent to which we own them and can punish them."

Hanley thought for a moment before saying, "That should work, Van. I see you've given this operation a lot of thought."

Morton smiled. "Don't forget, I used to work for Colonel Lawson. We had many conversations about the meaning of patriotism and its responsibilities."

"Obviously you were a good listener. Now then, I'd like you to formalize your threat narrative for me and show me the compromising intel you have on each of the eight principals."

"I believe you'll find everything you need in the envelope I just gave you."

"Once again, good job, Van. I'll call you if there's anything else I need."

CHAPTER 15

▼

The Following Evening at the Harrisons' House

When everyone was seated, John Harrison said, "Jack is going to brief us on the status of Operation Ice Breaker. Go ahead, Jack."

"Let me begin by saying I believe we're ready to execute this operation. Unless there are any up-front questions, I'll lead off by giving you the background facts we're working with."

There were no questions.

Hanley nodded. "First of all I want to acknowledge that Terry was right in saying Texas is ground zero for the Tea Party. Twelve of the forty Tea Party members in Congress are Texans, and of course, they're all white males. Ironically one of them represents Texas's First Congressional District—that's Charlie Wilson's old seat."

Harrison smiled. "Charlie was one of the most fascinating people I've had the opportunity to deal with. I'm sure you all remember how he single-handedly wrenched money from Congress to buy the Stinger missiles we delivered to the Afghan Mujahedeen rebels, which enabled them to drive out the Soviets. He was one of the very few civilians we ever recognized as an honorary member of the Clandestine Service."

Hanley nodded. "I remember him well. Charlie was a Democrat, and even though he represented a very conservative district, little about him was conservative. Of course, the current incumbent is no Charlie Wilson—not even close. Now let's get back to the big picture. One significant thing we discovered is that the Tea Party members are being asked to drink the Kool-Aid and are doing so with enthusiasm.

Most importantly, we learned how their caucus works. Let me explain. There are eight House Tea Party members, five of them Texans, who function as coordinators for the caucus. Each of them has four other caucus members they direct. The eight principals get their instructions via smartphones, generally from Senator Mayhem. He often schedules caucus meetings, sets forth the meeting's agenda, and then presides over them. Any questions so far?"

Harrison looked around, noted that there were no questions, and motioned for Hanley to continue.

Hanley nodded and said, "Our research, therefore, focused on the eight principals and Senator Mayhem. After learning how their caucus operated, we dug into their personal lives. In doing so we found each of them has enough compromising secrets to make them vulnerable to blackmail. And we've recorded five of them having illicit sex."

With a broad smile, Lawson said, "Does Thurston know that?"

"He certainly does."

Harrison nodded. "How do you intend to execute Operation Ice Breaker, Jack?"

Hanley nodded. "Our first action will be to communicate directly with the eight principals. In our communications we'll indict them for attempting to bring down the administration and, in the process, doing irreparable damage to our democracy and to the people of this country. That indictment will be accompanied by a cease-and-desist order regarding their obstructionism. They'll be told that their malicious and irresponsible governance has consequences. We'll be specific in the punitive action we'll take if they fail to both end the government shutdown and extend the debt limit indefinitely. The eight principals will then be directed to share our threat with their foot soldiers. To close the deal, each of the eight leaders, plus Senator Mayhem, will receive a summary of their transgressions and the warning that they'll be made public if they fail to follow our directions."

Harrison nodded. "That works for me. Do the rest of you have any comments or questions?"

Lawson raised a finger. "Are you also prepared to make physical threats if they fail to act as directed?"

Hanley nodded. "We gave a lot of thought to that and decided to be explicit and tough, so the answer to your question is yes. We'll tell them that if at any time they're obstructing the democratic processes of this country, they'll be considered anarchists and political terrorists. And we'll explain the range of punishments for those crimes. In general the punishment will fit the crime. If, for example, their obstructionism results in a dysfunctional government that impoverishes people or lets them die for lack of medical care, they stand to lose all their personal funds, their political careers, and potentially their lives. And we'll caution them that their financial sugar daddies will not be able to protect them."

"Well done, Jack," Lawson said. "That should do the job. How soon can you implement?"

"As soon as I'm authorized to, so to get authorization I'm handing each of you two sheets of paper. The first is the script of the communication we intend to make to the eight leaders. The second is a compilation of each of their indiscretions. Look these over and let me know if you approve."

After a minute or so, Harrison said, "I like it, Jack."

A few moments later, each of the others indicated their approval.

Hanley smiled. "Good. The second phase of Operation Ice Breaker begins tomorrow."

"Now we wait," Jennifer said. "We won't know whether Ice Breaker worked or not until the next floor vote. And that could be several days from now. My sense, however, is that the Tea Party has the Speaker by the balls—if he has any—and will ask him for a vote on ending the shutdown in the very near future."

Lawson nodded. "I agree, but the real test comes when the bill to extend the debt limit hits the floor. I suspect by then the people controlling Senator Mayhem will be blaming him for the Tea Party's retreat. Either way, we have to wait."

Harrison rapped his knuckles on the table and said, "There's no benefit to our sitting here and speculating. Our next meeting will be when we know the outcome of Ice Breaker. Until then, stay safe."

CHAPTER 16

▼

Two Weeks Later at the Harrisons' House

John Harrison asked for everyone's attention. He then lifted his champagne glass and said, "Here's to the success of Operation Ice Breaker."

"To Ice Breaker," the others responded.

"One hell of a job, Jack," Lawson said. "Be sure to give your people a serious pat on the back."

Hanley nodded. "It was just a matter of everyone doing their job."

"Don't be modest, Jack," Jennifer said. "Your team is good, but you're outstanding."

Hanley blushed. "Come on, Jennifer, you know damn well it was just routine business for us." After a moment he cocked his head and said, "Why do I have the feeling you have something more lined up for me?"

Jennifer smiled. "See, I said you were good. You'll get an answer to that question when we convene in the secure room."

Hanley nodded. "To cope with the suspense, I need another glass of champagne. Care to join me?"

"Naturally, I think we all will."

Once again the glasses were raised in a toast, this time to the future of their quiet revolution.

When everyone was seated, Harrison said, "I believe the success of Ice Breaker positions us nicely to devote our full attention to

Operation TBT. Since Terry has the lead on this one, I'll turn the meeting over to him."

Lawson, looking a bit grim, said, "It would be difficult for me to overstate the importance of achieving success in this operation. I believe if we fail in Texas, the future of our revolution is dim. Without putting too fine a point on it, I feel it's imperative we destroy the Texas roots of our national corruption. If we don't accomplish that, we have no hope of reforming Congress. But as I've said many times, if we gain control of Texas, we can break the stranglehold their politicians have had—and do have—on the federal government. And if we can flip Texas, we should be able to do the same to the other red states. So I'm recommending we go all in on TBT."

Jennifer interrupted. "On many occasions you've pointed out that historically Texas has been owned and operated by wealthy, horny, and hypocritical white males. How can we change that?"

"Good question, Jennifer. The flip answer is, replace them with women and other minorities. Interestingly, the serious answer is much the same. For too many years now Texas's minorities, especially women, have had little say in the operation of their state. And as a result they've been treated like second-class citizens. So I'm sure the women of Texas are more than a little frustrated and angry."

Jennifer nodded. "I've read that there's been a noticeable increase in the number of women and Hispanics who are politically active. Do you think this is a trend?"

"I think it's more than a trend. I think it's the beginning of a serious movement. For instance there's a progressive woman running for governor on the Democratic ticket who has a decent chance of winning, especially if she gets some help. As for the Hispanics, they now have strong leadership in the Castro brothers, both of whom are national celebrities. Their success story, which exemplifies the American dream, should encourage more Hispanics to become politically active."

Harrison raised a finger. "So you believe there are enough credible women and Hispanics seeking major offices in Texas to be elected by frustrated women and Hispanics. Is that right?"

Lawson nodded. "Yes, I think it's a distinct possibility, John. But it all hinges on them turning out to vote. Don't forget, historically in

Texas only about 25 percent of the women and Hispanics vote, which is understandable since they seldom have a dog in the fight."

"But you think they'll vote this time, right?"

Lawson shook his head. "Not necessarily. I expect they'll only vote if they're sufficiently informed and pissed off. And that's where we come in. We have to ensure that every progressive candidate speaks to the needs of women and Hispanics and angers them enough to vote."

Jennifer nodded. "So what's the plan?"

"It starts with the distribution of Thurston's book. As most of you know, I spent last week at Thurston's place reviewing his manuscript, and I think it's dynamite. His protagonist, Christian Malloy, reveals that the ingrained corruption of the Texas and federal governments is sponsored in large part by Big Oil. In the process Malloy details the role of the Koch brothers in sponsoring the Tea Party to carry out their anarchistic objectives. Malloy states that his primary reason for writing his exposés is to inform the voting public that America can no longer afford the corrupted Republican Party. Malloy then issues a call to duty for the ultra wealthy progressives in this country. He asks them to put their money where their patriotism is."

Harrison smiled. "That sounds good, but how will Thurston's book help in Operation TBT?"

Lawson nodded. "In addition to writing about the perverted politics in Texas, Thurston offers advice to the Texas Democratic organizations on how to run winning campaigns and get-out-the-vote operations. He also points out that a key to winning in Texas is having the funds needed to run aggressive campaigns and to neutralize the conservative media there. Again he makes a plea for the wealthy patriots of Texas to put their money to work in freeing Texas from the clutches of Big Oil."

Harrison smiled. "Sounds like Thurston's book will do the trick. And I love it when a plan comes together."

Lawson held up his hand and said, "Hey, there's still a lot of work to do, John. Phil, we'll need you to get Thurston's book published and distributed as soon as practical. We also need you to set up some dummy corporations to finance the Texas PACs. And it would be helpful if your people could develop some TV ads for Texas candidates. Ads that scare the hell out of their voters by disclosing the damage their Republican congressmen have done and will continue to do if they're not replaced."

Jennifer nodded. "Since the most recent government shutdown cost the country more than twenty-four billion dollars, it cost every single Texan more than eight hundred dollars."

"That's good stuff, Jennifer, thank you," Lawson said. "Now then, are there any questions?"

After thinking for a moment Harrison said, "How do you intend to pursue Operation TBT?"

"Lan and I will be going back to San Antonio to set up a base of operations for TBT. While we're there, we'll work with Charlie Garcia to accomplish two things. First we'll arrange for the widest possible distribution of Thurston's book. Second, we'll get involved in raising as much money as we can."

"Will you make yourselves visible to the Democratic politicians and organizations there?"

"Only to the degree Garcia thinks it's appropriate. My intention at this point is to simply present myself as a wealthy representative of a wealthy group of patriots who want Texas turned blue. So while Charlie is handling the political aspects, Lan and I'll try to infiltrate the social circle of some of San Antonio's wealthier Democrats. I understand many of them live in a very upscale subdivision called the Dominion. I also understand that some of those high rollers donated significant amounts to the president's reelection campaign. Given that, there's a possibility we can induce some of them to donate to the TBT movement as well. Lan will do what's necessary to encourage that generosity."

Jennifer smiled. "No doubt of that. She's always been a social charmer."

"*Merci*, Jennifer," Lan said. "It seems I'll finally have a tangible role in this revolution."

Harrison nodded. "There's no doubt fund-raising is key to the success of Operation TBT. So your role in helping get those funds is very important. In the meantime, keeping Terry functioning properly will be sufficient."

Lawson smiled and said, "Unless there are any questions, Lan and I will head back to McLean and start packing for our mission in San Antonio."

There were no questions.

CHAPTER 17

▼

A Week Later, San Antonio, Texas

Lan stood in the middle of the living room and looked around. "It's beautiful," she said. "We owe Congressman Garcia a dinner for getting it for us. I love both the floor plan and the furnishings—it's functional and attractive. It should work nicely for everyday living as well as entertaining."

Lawson smiled. "I agree. We were damn lucky to get it, even if it is just for a month or so. Charlie told me the owners are a wealthy couple with a large home in Rancho Mirage, California, and that they'll be there several weeks for health reasons. I gather they keep this large town house primarily for tax purposes. Charlie also mentioned that Stone Oak is the new Dominion, so we should have some upscale neighbors."

Lan nodded. "It seems perfect in every respect. And I understand it's a convenient location—that there are two wonderful shopping malls nearby loaded with upscale shops and good restaurants. I believe one is called the Rim and the other La Cantera. I can't wait to check them out."

Lawson smiled. "I'll be checking out the Rim tomorrow. I'm meeting Charlie there for a late breakfast. That reminds me, we need to do some grocery shopping if we intend to have dinner here this evening."

Lan looked surprised. "I thought with all the restaurants around here, I wouldn't have to do any cooking."

Lawson shook his head. "We've been eating out far too much recently. I'm ready for some serious home cooking."

"Do you mean that euphemistically or actually?"

"Both."

"So in addition to the basic stuff, we'll need some good wine and cheese. I understand the HEB stores have both."

After dinner that evening, the Lawsons retired to the den for coffee, Belgian truffles, and a little Judy Collins music. For several minutes nothing was said as they listened to "Send in the Clowns" and lapsed into a meditative state that lasted several minutes. The silence was finally broken when Lan softly sang, "What now, my love?"

Lawson looked up from his coffee and said, "It's a bit early for bed, don't you think?"

"That's not what I meant. I was inquiring as to what we do now that we're settled in this lovely house."

"My first thought still prevails . . . just a bit later."

Lan frowned, pursed her lips, and shook her head

After a moment, Lawson said, "Okay, since you've packed away your sense of humor, I'll be serious. At the top of my to-do list is having Charlie Garcia connect us to the political movers and shakers in San Antonio so we can appeal to their patriotism and get them to contribute to TBT."

"And you're looking for substantial contributions, *n'est pa?*"

"Of course, and the incentive is that my compatriots and I will match whatever amount they put in the pot."

"Where do I fit into this scenario?"

"No doubt it will take a little wining and dining to get much out of them. So you'll host a few intimate cocktail parties and dinners, while looking very seductive, of course."

"Shall I practice on you?"

"Please do."

"Okay, how's this. 'Oh, you're a good-looking man. Would you like to sleep with me tonight?'"

Lawson laughed. "Not too subtle, but it works for me. Let's check out our new bed."

"Not to hurry, my love. A blue pill first."

CHAPTER 18

▼

The Following Morning at Mimi's Café

After he and Garcia had placed their orders, Lawson said, "I'm glad you suggested Mimi's for our meeting. It's certainly convenient, and from what I can see of the food, it should be delicious."

Garcia smiled. "And it is. I think it's the best place in San Antonio for either breakfast or lunch. I come here as often as I can. And now that we're here, what did you want to talk about?"

Lawson nodded. "There are two things we need your help with. The first is in getting some recognition of a new book written by a best-selling author named Sidney Thurston. The second thing is to introduce me to the wealthy Democrats here in San Antonio who might be open to an attractive offer."

"Which is . . . . ?"

"The offer is that my colleagues and I will match whatever amount of money the locals contribute to the cause."

Garcia smiled. "I believe there are some here who would view that offer quite favorably."

"Good. Now let me explain my thinking on how we might go about this. In a week or so I'll have advance copies of Thurston's new book, a novel titled *Saving Democracy*. In it Thurston states that there are two major prerequisites to saving our threatened democracy. The first requisite is that the voting public must become fully informed as to the political realities of our times. The second prerequisite is that wealthy progressives must contribute as much as they can to counter the excessive financial resources of the Republican Party."

Garcia nodded. "I don't think anyone would dispute his premises. The question is, however, how does one accomplish those two things?"

Lawson smiled. "In my opinion Thurston does a great job of answering that question. To address the first requisite, he goes into exquisite detail on the different ways the public can be informed. For the second requisite, his appeal for help from wealthy progressives is both profound and poignant. He reminds them that it's their patriotic duty to help preserve our democracy. So I firmly believe Thurston's book could be the lynchpin that entices wealthy patriots to donate to the revolution, both here in Texas and nationwide."

Garcia nodded. "What makes you think his book will find traction here in Texas?"

"For the simple reason that much of Thurston's story is focused on how wealthy Texas oil men have historically created corrupt politicians here in Texas who were later shipped to Washington to do their bidding there. Even though the book is fiction, it's fact based and he names names. Most importantly, Thurston lays out in detail what needs to be done in Texas to free the state from Republican bondage."

Garcia smiled. "And you want prospective donors to see a copy. Is that right?"

Lawson nodded. "That's absolutely right. There's no question in my mind that any conscientious, patriotic-minded individual that reads the book will be anxious to join the fight."

"So how can I help?"

"One way would be to have a gala book-centered dinner for six or eight leading prospects. If those prospects were convinced to join the revolution, they might give copies of the book to wealthy friends, and so forth."

Garcia thought for a moment. "That makes sense. How and where could we hold such a dinner?"

"Lan and I could host it at our place. She's good at planning those kinds of affairs. She can arrange for the dinner to be catered, and I can arrange for a bartender."

Garcia nodded. "That sounds good. Now I have a suggestion. Let's limit the number of prospects to four. That would give us twelve at the table, making a single conversation easier."

"Good thought, Charlie. So here's what I suggest. I'll have copies of the book in just a few days. So when you initiate the invitations, you can tell them they'll receive a copy of Thurston's book at the dinner. It'll be my job, representing Thurston, to give them a preview of the book and make a pitch for their participation in his crusade."

"Would it be possible for Thurston himself to be there?"

Lawson chuckled. "I'm afraid not. Sidney Thurston is a nom de plume, a pen name the author is using to hide his identity."

"But I believe you said this was something of a sequel to Thurston's first book, *A Cancer on Democracy.*"

Lawson smiled. "It's rather complicated, but I'll try to explain. After *Cancer* was published, there were two attempts made on Thurston's life. That forced him to assume a new identity and disappear from public view. Now the man formerly known as Sidney Thurston did, in fact, write this sequel, *Saving Democracy.* But in order for him to remain anonymous, I have to represent him in every respect. And the fact is I can talk about any aspect of the book since I was with him when he wrote it."

"You're right, Terry, it's complicated, but I do understand. If asked, I'll simply say the author isn't available to sign books, but his agent is."

Lawson nodded. "That should be sufficient to get us started with fund-raising. But there's also another task I need your help with."

"And what is that?"

"I need your help in getting the book in the hands of the Democratic leadership in Texas and in Washington. Can you help me do that?"

Garcia thought for a few seconds before saying, "I can write letters of transmittal and furnish addresses, but I can't handle the mailing part."

Lawson smiled. "That's all I need, since we're doing the distribution mailings from Northern Virginia."

Garcia nodded. "Now back to task one. How soon do you want to hold the fund-raising dinner?"

"I should receive a carton of books in just a few days. So let's schedule the dinner for a week from Saturday. That should be enough lead time to make the arrangements and issue invitations."

Garcia smiled. "I agree. Now then, that's enough planning for today, Terry. It's time for you to experience Mimi's wonderful cuisine."

CHAPTER 19

▼

Saturday Night, Twelve Days Later at the Lawsons' Town House

Charlie Garcia and his wife greeted each of the four couples as they arrived and introduced them to the Lawsons. First to arrive were George McAllister, a lawyer, and his wife. Minutes later Kyle Anderson and his wife arrived. Anderson, Lawson had been told, had inherited a fortune from his banker father and was a successful investment banker himself. Close behind the Andersons were James Wakefield, a real estate developer and his wife. The last to arrive were Hector and Peggy Rodriguez. Rodriguez was identified to Lawson as the CEO of a prosperous technology company. Lawson noted that the men were uniformly dressed in dark pinstriped business suits and the ladies in long dresses. *A dignified group*, he thought.

After the Lawsons engaged in a brief get-acquainted chat with each couple as they arrived, the men were directed to the bar to get champagne or an alternative drink for themselves and their spouses. Meanwhile Lan escorted the ladies into the living room to make themselves comfortable.

With everyone congregated in the living room, sipping their drinks and chatting, two young serving women in short-skirted French-maid outfits began to circulate with trays of shrimp and other appetizers. Lawson was amused to see that as the young women passed by, the men shifted their gazes from Lan to them. Since Lawson had been briefed about the men's social proclivities, he felt optimistic about being able to do business with them.

Thirty minutes and several drinks later, dinner was announced. Hearing the call, everyone meandered to the dining room where they found name cards directing them to their place at the table. The arrangement, planned to facilitate conversation, had the Lawsons seated at either end of the table; Charlie Garcia to Terry's left and his wife to Lan's left; the McAllisters and the Wakefields on Charlie's side of the table; and the Andersons and Rodriguezes across from them. Everyone seemed happy with the arrangement.

During the first course of salad greens and hearts of palm topped with a champagne vinaigrette dressing, the conversation was subdued and innocuous. Admiration was expressed by some for the appetizer wine, a 2005 Pouilly Fusse. As the meal progressed and the wine disappeared, the four guest couples began exchanging amusing tidbits of gossip regarding recent parties at the Dominion. Lan and Lawson exchanged smiles when the gossip turned a bit titillating.

Nearing the end of the main course, the conversation shifted from the Chicken Scaloppini Veronique and accompanying 1996 Bourgogne Pinot Noir, to local politics and questions regarding Sidney Thurston's book. At this point Lawson seized control of the conversation by saying, "Before I tell you about Thurston's book, I'd like to thank you for being here this evening. It's been delightful getting to know you. So Lan and I are especially grateful you're here especially since you know the purpose of this dinner. Now then, how many of you know anything about Sidney Thurston or his latest book, *Saving Democracy*?"

McAllister and Wakefield raised their hands partway and McAllister said, "I read Thurston's *A Cancer on Democracy* a few years ago and liked it. But all I know about his new book is what I heard from Charlie, so I'm anxious to read it."

Lawson nodded. "Good, because you'll be taking home a copy tonight. But for the purpose of discussion now, what did Charlie tell you?"

McAllister nodded and said, "Charlie thinks Thurston makes a strong case for the necessity of having to break the stranglehold Republicans have on Congress and our statehouse. Charlie also said that Thurston acknowledged it will take a substantial infusion of money to counter what the Republicans have."

Lawson nodded. "Does that sound reasonable to you?"

McAllister hesitated before saying, "There's no doubt Republicans need to be purged from both Congress and our statehouse. But I for one will be reluctant to contribute anything substantial unless I know the details of how the money will be spent. Too many Texas Democrats seem to have a problem managing money."

Lawson smiled. "I've heard that myself. So I think you'll be more than pleased when you read the advice Thurston gives the Democratic leadership here. I think you'll also be pleased when I tell you how friends of mine and myself will be contributing to the financing of the Turn Texas Blue movement and, in the process, controlling how the money is allocated and spent."

McAllister nodded and said, "That means I need to read the book right away. I think we all do, and if you're right, Terry, we'll need to meet again to work out the details of how we can contribute to the movement."

Lawson nodded. "What do you propose?"

"I propose that that you, Charlie, and the four of us meet next Saturday at my club. We can gather at noon and have lunch before starting our business meeting."

Lawson nodded and the other four followed suit. Seeing this, he said, "Now then, shall we have dessert?"

Lan cocked her head and said, "It's about time, dear. We ladies have been waiting."

Lawson smiled and signaled one of the waiters standing alongside the buffet at the end of the room that he should ignite the chafing dish they were tending. He did, and when the burst of flames subsided, the hot cherries jubilee was spooned atop dishes of French vanilla ice cream and quickly served. At the same time, each guest's flute was filled with Veuve Clicquot champagne.

Ten minutes later, Kyle Anderson raised his glass and said, "Here's to the Lawsons for this delightful evening."

"To the Lawsons," the others chanted while consuming the last of their champagne.

After leaving the table, the guests congregated in the living room for demitasse espresso and chocolates. Thirty minutes later, the couples began their exodus. When the last of them left, Lawson said, "Well done, dear. I think we're in."

CHAPTER 20

▼

Noon the Following Saturday, at the Dominion Golf Club

After lunch in the casual Hogan Room, the six men repaired to a private meeting room on the second level. When everyone was comfortably seated, George McAllister said, "We're here today to discuss Sidney Thurston's book *Saving Democracy* and get answers to any questions we have. As you know, Terry represents Thurston and is qualified to answer any of your questions."

"Thanks, George," Lawson said. "First off, have all of you read the book?"

All four nodded so Lawson said, "Good. Now the reason I'm here speaking with you is that my friends and I fully subscribe to Thurston's view that our democracy is in great peril and that our nation is spiraling down into mediocrity at the hands of corrupt politicians. So we've vowed to take whatever action is necessary to clean up Congress and restore the morality and values that once made our country great. In short, we're engaged in a revolution to rid the country of corrupt politicians, as well as those corrupting them. But our revolution requires extensive support, and that's why I'm talking to you. Any questions so far?"

Kyle Anderson raised a finger. "Is this a generic revolution or are you targeting individuals?"

"That's a good question, and the answer is both. We're generically attacking the Republican Party because in recent years its members have operated in lockstep to support the needs of the wealthy while neglecting the needs of the middle and working classes. But we're also targeting corrupt individuals in both the public and private sectors. These targets are individuals who habitually deceive the American people to further their own greedy objectives. An example of such an individual is the president of the NRA."

Anderson shook his head. "I'm not sure that's a good example, Terry. You're now in serious gun country. There are a goodly number of Texans who want nothing more than a pickup truck and a collection of guns."

Lawson smiled. "I understand that. But like most Americans owning guns, they're conscientious about how they use them. Now the president of the NRA would have you believe that the membership of the NRA wants no controls whatsoever over gun purchases and usage, which is totally false. The NRA was founded to promote gun safety, and 68 percent of the current membership believes there should be stringent background checks for the purchase of any gun. That's one of the reasons the president of the NRA has to go."

Anderson nodded. "I see. Is it fair for me to assume you have the capability of collecting incriminating information about individuals you want gone?"

"Yes, you can assume that."

"Would you care to tell us how you manage that?"

"No."

McAllister chuckled. "You know very well, Kyle, there's a reason a magician never reveals his secrets. Now then, Terry, I have a question: What do you know about me?"

"What would you like to know?"

"That was a serious question, Terry."

Lawson smiled. "I know you donated a substantial amount of money to the president's campaign, and that tells me everything I need to know about you."

"And the same answer for the other three?"

"Yes. You've all put your concern for the welfare of this country ahead of coddling your wealth. In my eyes that makes you patriots."

"Are you looking for something more than money from us?" Wakefield asked.

Lawson nodded. "Let me reiterate how we expect our revolution to unfold. Ultimately Congress has to be reformed, but that's a long-term task. So our most immediate objective is to rid Congress of as many Republicans as possible in the 2014 elections. In the process, however, we'll attempt to turn as many red states blue as possible, beginning with Texas."

Looking puzzled, Husted said, "Why Texas?"

"There are a number of reasons. First because it's the cradle of the corruption that now paralyzes Washington. Second because it is, and has been for some time, a horribly managed state. Third because it has a significant number of congressmen, and finally because it's a big, slow-moving target."

McAllister drew back his head. "Are you putting down the great state of Texas?"

Lawson laughed. "The perception that Texas is a great state is an illusion perpetuated by Big Oil and the military-industrial complex because it is a great state for them. But with Texas being forty-ninth in education, fiftieth in public health, and fiftieth in environmental protection, the majority of Texans suffer. So for them, the state is anything but great."

They all smiled and nodded. Then Anderson said, "We fully understand and agree with what you just said. Unfortunately the illusion of Texas being a great state is good for our economy and good for us businesspeople."

Lawson nodded. "I know, but think how much better it would be for you businesspeople if that were a reality. Think how much more money the majority of Texans would spend if they had excess income beyond that needed for basic survival. And the glaring fact is that Texas has the potential to be a great state for everyone, not just the wealthy. And that's why I'm here talking to you."

McAllister smiled. "Your point is well taken, Terry. So what's your plan for bailing out Texas?"

Lawson nodded. "The simplistic answer is by regaining the legislature and the governor's office. But that only begs the question of how. But before I explain the how of our plan, let me tell what knowledgeable pundits are saying. There's consensus that turning Texas blue is a steep hill to climb. Several reasons are cited. One is that the Republican organizations are too deeply entrenched and that their candidates are too heavily subsidized. Another reason is that Democrats have too small a donor base and their voter appeal is too narrow. Unfortunately all those reasons are valid."

Wakefield nodded. "So what makes you optimistic?"

"There's a saying that goes something like this: 'If you understand the problem, you can find a way to solve it,' and from my professional experience, I know that's true. So here's how we solve each of the problems Texas Democrats have. First and foremost, Texas Democrats need more donors and more money to offset the advantage Big Oil and other industrial contributors give the Republicans. That means recruiting more donors who can make larger contributions."

"I gather that's where we come in," McAllister said.

Lawson nodded. "Yes, it is, so let me explain. My colleagues and I believe it will take a minimum of thirty million to offset what we think Big Oil and the Koch brothers will bring to the party in 2014. So my colleagues and I are prepared to put up at least fifteen million in matching funds for whatever is raised here in Texas. And our hope is that you four will start the ball rolling, first by donating, and then by recruiting other contributors. And when enough major contributors have been recruited here in San Antonio, have you extend your fund-raising efforts to other urban locales such as Houston and Dallas."

McAllister nodded. "We can get things going here in San Antonio, but I don't see how we could do much of anything in Houston or Dallas."

Lawson smiled. "I'll bet this club has reciprocal privileges with clubs in those other two cities. Checking them out would be a start."

Anderson laughed. "That's true, but the clubs in Houston and Dallas are rather exclusive—oil men only."

Lawson shook his head. "Okay, but keep in mind how effective Thurston's plea is for wealthy progressive patriots to do the right thing. So when you're dealing with prospective donors, have them read his book—just as you did."

McAllister nodded. "I think we have the idea. How much are you looking for from us?"

"That's for you to decide, but obviously the more, the better. I suggest you think of it as pump priming. For instance, if each of you contributed two hundred fifty thousand dollars, that, plus our matching funds, would give the state's Democratic Committee two million to work with right away. That would give the Turn Texas Blue movement a powerful boost."

Wakefield nodded. "I for one can handle a quarter mil. So how do I go about making a contribution?"

Lawson smiled. "Thanks, James. To answer your question, we're setting up PACs to which you can wire transfer your donations. And remember, they'll be matched that same day. Also keep in mind that Charlie will control the allocation of funds from the PACs. So just tell him if you have any preferences as to how you want the money used."

Anderson raised a finger and said, "I'll contribute the same as James."

When Rodriguez and McAllister indicated they would follow suit, Lawson said, "A very profound thank-you to you, gentlemen. In my mind you'll be remembered as the patriots who fired the first figurative shots in Texas's modern revolution."

CHAPTER 21

▼

Three Days Later, the Palm Restaurant, San Antonio, Texas

As soon as Garcia was seated, Lawson said, "What would you like to drink, Charlie?"

"I think I'll join you with a dry vodka martini."

"Good," Lawson said as he motioned for the waiter to bring another like his. "Do you think there's daylight at the end of the tunnel?"

Garcia shook his head. "Maybe a glimmer, but that's all. I think the Turn Texas Blue movement has potential, but at this time it doesn't seem to have a winning game plan."

Lawson nodded. "That's understandable because it's still early in the game. Obviously the leadership needs both money and direction. I think we've started the ball rolling in raising funds, and Thurston's book is available to give them motivation and direction."

Again Garcia shook his head. "If you check their website, you'll see that they're organized just as they have been for years. It's unlikely they'll be able to expand either their donor base or their voter base."

"I think you're too pessimistic, Charlie. I believe the cadre of patriots we've recruited will help broaden the donor base, and the women candidates running for state office will help broaden the voter base."

"I hope you're right, Terry. But the political insiders I've been talking to think the entrenched Republicans are safe for at least four more years. They have both the money and the organization to protect their incumbents."

Lawson smiled. "So they're cocky, which means they're vulnerable."

"They're cocky for a reason, and if they're vulnerable, I don't see it."

"I do. On one hand, they're vulnerable because they don't expect any organized opposition. On the other hand, they're vulnerable because my colleagues have the means to expose all their dirty secrets. Going public with that sort of information should put them on the defensive."

Garcia nodded. "Of course, Thurston has already revealed some of those secrets, which leaves me to wonder how many Texans will have read his book before the next election."

Lawson shook his head. "I expect not that many. But the more pertinent question to ask is, how many will have seen the movie based on his book?"

Garcia drew back his head. "So that's the grand plan. It sounds good, but I wonder what the odds are that *Saving Democracy* will make it to the big screen?"

Lawson smiled. "I think the chances are rather good. There are a lot of talented progressives in the movie industry who want to see the government reformed."

Garcia smiled. "Do you have a plan for getting that done?"

"The plan isn't completely formed yet, but we're starting by sending books to leading screenplay writers like Aaron Sorkin and leading producers such as Robert Woodward, George Clooney, George Lucas, and Oliver Stone. All these talented people have recognized, in one way or another, the urgent need for reforming the government."

Garcia nodded. "Do you think there's time?"

"I do and for two reasons. The first is because Thurston wrote his book in a way that will make it easy for conversion into a screenplay. The second reason is that Hollywood is geared up to quickly crank out contemporary movies not requiring elaborate sets or costumes."

"I hope you're right, Terry, because that seems the only way of effectively informing the general public."

After thinking for a few moments, Lawson said, "Something that wouldn't hurt, Charlie, is to get the book reviewed by the *San*

Antonio Express News. I've read the paper every day and am impressed with its editorial staff. Every editorial I've read has been insightful, intelligent, and articulately written. So I suspect someone there might be interested in Thurston's book."

"You may be right, Terry. For the 2012 election, the *Express News* endorsed practically the entire Democratic ticket. So I'll see what I can do to get a copy to one of their senior editors."

"One more thing, Charlie, how much of an impact do you think the Castro brothers will have in turning Texas blue?"

Garcia smiled. "That's hard to say. Joaquin is currently busy in Congress trying to get some badly needed legislation passed, and Julian was recently reelected mayor. Now there's no question both of them are destined to be superstars in Washington, but it's unclear how much influence they'll have on Texas politics in the near term. However, one of my omniscient political friends predicts Julian will be elected governor in four years and from that office begin making major changes to the political landscape of Texas."

Lawson nodded. "Thanks, Charlie, I understand. There is a way, however, that either or both of them could share their star power, and that's by endorsing Dem candidates at rallies and in TV ads."

Garcia smiled. "I'm sure they'll do that. And while I'm thinking about it, Joaquin ran a near perfect campaign to win his seat in Congress. When the election was over, very few people knew the name of his opponent since it was never mentioned during the campaign. I knew that would please you since that's what you preach."

Lawson laughed. "I believe that's what Thurston preaches."

"Of course, but he got the idea from someone, didn't he?"

"It's possible he got it from me because I never hesitate to say it's the most important of the campaign fundamentals."

Garcia nodded. "All the more reason you should be impressed with the Castros. Not only are they bright and charismatic, they're also intuitive politicians."

Lawson nodded. "There's no doubt they're ready for prime time, it's just unfortunate they're not currently positioned to be much help in taking back Texas."

Garcia smiled. "Don't worry, Terry. If we're not successful in this election, we certainly will be in 2016. I suspect we'll have a woman at the top of the presidential ticket who'll be looking for a bright young Texas Hispanic as a running mate."

Lawson chuckled. "I think you've got it Charlie. So if nothing else, our efforts now will set the stage for a presidential sweep in '16."

Garcia nodded. "That's my expectation. So we need to keep pushing hard now in spite of how difficult it looks."

Lawson nodded. "I was hoping to hear you say that, because I need to get back to Virginia."

"I understand," Garcia said. "I suppose you and your colleagues will be busy distributing and promoting Thurston's book."

"That's our main task for a while, but we'll also be devoting time and energy to ensuring that the national Democratic organizations are all using Thurston's playbook."

Garcia nodded, pulled a large manila envelope from his briefcase and said, "Here are the names, addresses, and letters of transmission you asked for. That should help you and your colleagues put most of the Democratic organizations on the same page."

"Thanks, Charlie. We really appreciate all you've done. You have my number, so if there's anything you need, don't hesitate to call. Oh, and the Take Back Texas PAC now has two million for you to work with."

Garcia smiled. "Many thanks. I'll ensure the money is used wisely."

CHAPTER 22

▼

Three Days Later at the Harrisons' House: John and Jennifer Harrison greeted each of their arriving colleagues with a glass of champagne. When everyone was congregated, Harrison raised his glass and said. "Let's toast the Lawsons and welcome them back from the Western frontier."

Everyone clicked glasses and said, "Welcome back."

Lawson smiled. "We're certainly glad to be back, but Texas is not as primitive as you might think. In fact San Antonio is downright civilized. We enjoyed being there, and I believe we accomplished a lot."

Harrison held up a hand and said, "Terry and Lan will be telling us more about their trip once we're secluded. For the time being let's just enjoy the champagne and catch up on our personal activities."

Jennifer smiled and said, "I'll go first. John and I continue to appreciate our seclusion here. We work out every day, eat healthy, and do a great deal of reading. Okay, Phil, what about you?"

"I'm busier than ever so most of my social life is between ten at night and five in the morning. Most of that time is spent sleeping with my wife."

Jennifer nodded. "So how much sleep do you get?"

"No comment."

"Okay then, Jack, it's your turn."

Hanley shook his head. "My life is the same as Phil's, except no wife to sleep with. The extent of my interaction with the opposite sex is thirty seconds of banter with my secretary in the morning. That keeps me turned off for the rest of the day."

Jennifer laughed. "It sounds like we should refer your case to the Salvation Army."

Hanley looked puzzled. "Why is that?"

"Because the Salvation Army serves the needy."

"Very funny."

Jennifer smiled. "I thought so. Now then we can defer hearing from the Lawsons until we're behind closed doors. I'm sure they have a great deal to share with us."

When everyone was seated, Harrison turned the meeting over to Lawson.

Lawson nodded and said, "As you know, Lan and I went to San Antonio to organize and launch Operation TBT. In a sense we succeeded in doing that. However, the outlook for taking back Texas in 2014 is not all that bright. Here are a few of the salient facts. The downside is that the Republican Party is deeply entrenched in Texas and has whatever amount of money is needed to keep it that way. Conversely, the Democratic Party has little or no presence in many of the rural counties, has too narrow a donor base, and has too little appeal to voters other than minorities. The only plus for Democrats is the fact that they are moving to correct these deficiencies."

Harrison raised a finger and said, "So should we abandon Operation TBT?"

Lawson shook his head. "No. As I just said, there's movement by the Democrats to correct their problems, and with our help those movements should gain momentum. Expanded fund-raising has started, and with women candidates running for top offices, including the governor's, the voter base should broaden out. Historically only 25 percent of women and Hispanics vote. So if those percentages can be jacked up, it'll make a big difference."

Harrison shook his head. "But it won't be enough to flip Texas, right?"

"It's unlikely in 2014. In 2016, however, it could be an entirely different story."

"And why is that?"

"There are several reasons. First, the Democratic Party in Texas will be better organized, better funded and more proactive in getting out the vote. Second, more quality women and Hispanics will be candidates, and third because the all-star Castro brothers will be in play. In addition, they expect it'll be a woman heading up the Democratic presidential ticket, and that she'll win in a national landslide that includes Texas."

Jennifer smiled and said, "I think they're right, and I believe the woman's name is Hillary. I also believe she'll have an easy time of it since the all-male Republican leadership has dug itself an awfully deep hole and has no viable candidate to oppose her. They've pretty well run out of white WASP celebrity phonies like Reagan, McCain, W. Bush, and Romney."

"They certainly believe that in Texas," Lawson said. "In fact Garcia expects Hillary's running mate to be one of the Castro brothers, probably Julian."

Harrison nodded. "I have to agree, the prospect for 2016 looks bright. So do we tread water in Texas until then?"

Lawson shook his head. "No. My recommendation is that we immediately focus on the task of rooting out every damn Texas Tea Party representative now serving in Congress."

Hanley raised a finger and said, "As you know we already have compromising information on four of them. And it won't take too much additional effort to compromise the other five."

Harrison nodded "That's good, Jack. So continue Operation Ice Breaker until we have enough to bury the whole damn Tea Party. So thank you, Terry and Lan, for a job well done in Texas. Now then, let's turn our attention to our set-piece operation—Operation Movie Time. I know everyone is aware that it's especially important for us to get Thurston's book onto the big screen. If we fail to do that we'll have a bitch of a job trying to adequately inform the voting public. So it's imperative we devote as much attention and resources as possible to getting that done."

Lawson nodded. "There's no question about that, John. So who has the lead on this one?"

The Harrisons exchanged glances before Jennifer said, "John and I discussed this and decided you and Lan would be perfect for the job. After all it was your idea and you are Thurston's guiding light and agent aren't you?"

Lawson frowned. "What about Operation TBT?

Harrison nodded. "You've successfully launched it and it's now in maintenance mode. We've shipped the case of books you requested for Garcia, and Phil continues to transfer funds to our PACs there. So other than occasionally conveying Jack's intelligence to Garcia, you should have nothing more to do for TBT."

After pausing for several moments, Lawson said, "Okay, Lan and I will take the lead, but we're going to need help from Phil and Jack."

Harrison nodded. "What kind of help?"

"First of all, we need help in obtaining intelligence on the movers and shakers in the movie industry. Getting a book in front of the major players is difficult at best. You have to know who has both access and influence with them. Once you know that the next step is getting to that individual with an offer he or she will find difficult to refuse."

Hanley raised a finger. "I can certainly get the intelligence you need, and I assume Phil can see to the offer-making."

Martin nodded. "Of course I can. We have more than a little experience in doing that sort of thing. More immediately, however, if Terry is going to function as Thurston's agent he'll need an agency to operate from. I'll take care of that."

Lawson smiled. "Good. Now the first thing we need to do is get creditable reviews for the book, but that shouldn't be too difficult. After all Thurston is a best-selling author. The only trick here is that the reviews have to be uniformly glowing, which might require a little incentive for one or two of them."

Jennifer cocked her head. "But you think the book is solid, don't you?"

"Of course, but every parent thinks their child is perfect. Besides, different reviewers have different perspectives on what makes a book good. So what I'm suggesting is that it wouldn't hurt to ensure that the major reviewers come out with similar laudatory reviews."

Harrison smiled. "It never hurts to have the game fixed. So what's your next step, Terry?"

Lawson nodded. "Lan and I'll work with the publisher to see what their promotion plans are. At minimum I would expect a press release to the news media trumpeting the return of best-selling author Sidney Thurston with another bombshell that rips away the shroud of corruption now crippling the government."

Jennifer laughed. "Sounds like you're ready to write the press release yourself."

"Yeah, if need be. Now then, after that we monitor the media's response and cherry-pick the laudatory reviews for use in getting reviews from prestigious national review organizations. Their reviews will give us the fodder for media ads and letters of introduction to leading Hollywood agents. After that we send copies of the book to the producers of Comedy Central's *Daily Show*, as well as the producers of MSNBC's evening shows. Reviews by them would likely generate buzz for the book on the social networks."

Harrison nodded. "I'm with you so far, but I'm wondering how all that will get the book onto the big screen."

"All that, John, will do two things. First it will sell books, and second it will create an ever expanding audience for the movie version. Once that's done it should be relatively easy to find agents with Hollywood connections. In the meantime Jack and Phil will identify the people closest to the progressive producers whose production companies are most likely to fast track Thurston's book to the big screen. Once those people are identified, as Thurston's agent I'll make contact with them with offers they'll find hard to refuse."

Harrison nodded. "Hell, sweeten the pot enough and I might produce the movie myself."

Jennifer shook her head. "John, you don't have a clue as to how a movie is produced."

"You seem to forget, my dear, that a few years ago we produced a movie called *Argo*."

Jennifer frowned and said, "That was an agency operation that you had nothing to do with. And no movie was produced, there was only the illusion of a movie being produced."

Lawson interrupted. "Would you two mind if I continued."

"Sorry, Terry, go ahead."

"Thank you," Lawson said. "My expectation is that several producers will show interest. If that's the case we can go with the one with the best track record. Now then, that's the extent of the game plan I have at this time. Are there any questions?"

Hanley nodded. "You mentioned needing contact information for various people. Are you aware that that information is available to anybody on the Internet?"

"Yes, and I'm also aware that most of it is useless. Here's the deal. Let's say I want to send a copy of Thurston's book to Aaron Sorkin. I get online and discover that Sorkin has a mailing address in Scarsdale, New York, where he grew up. But he also has three other mailing addresses. Now which one do I mail the book to? But it really doesn't matter where I send it, because Sorkin won't see it anyway. That's because he has an office staff somewhere that screens his nonpersonal mail. So it's that key person on his staff to whom I want to send the book and the one I need contact information for."

Hanley nodded. "Got it, so are you going to give me a list of everyone you want to see the book?"

"Indeed, and I'll have that for you in a couple of days."

With that, Harrison adjourned the meeting.

CHAPTER 23

▼

Two Days Later, CIA Headquarters, Langley, Virginia: "Good morning, Janice," Lawson said, "Is he as testy as ever?"

"Of course, he never changes. And how are you this morning, Mr. Lawson?"

"Good enough to put up with your boss for a few minutes."

"Would a cup of coffee help?"

"I hope so, and make it black please."

Janice nodded and said, "Go on in, he's expecting you. I'll bring the coffee in a minute."

When Lawson stepped into his office, Hanley looked up and said, "Good morning, Terry, have a seat. Do you want some coffee?"

Before Lawson could answer, Janice came through the door and set his coffee on the desk in front of him. He smiled and said, "Thank you, Janice."

Hanley looked puzzled. "Do you two have something going?"

"No, it's just the result of a little courtesy, Jack. You might try it someday."

Hanley frowned. "I have and it doesn't work for me. Now what do you have for me?"

"It's a list of people that need to see Thurston's book. But I've been thinking."

"And . . . ?"

"I was thinking about the most feasible way of getting the attention of one of the progressive movie producers."

"So what did you decide?"

"Based on some research I did, it looks impossible to get the book directly into the hands of one of the big four progressive producers. I did discover, however, that major movie production companies use either an in-house or a freelance reviewer to find promising screenplays or books. So it's those individuals I need to employ in order to get Thurston's book looked at by one or more of the big boys."

"And you want me to find one of those reviewers, right?"

"Find one or more, yes."

"Okay, that's a job for Van," Hanley said before hitting the intercom and asking his secretary to have Morton come to his office as soon as possible.

Lawson smiled. "It's good to see that Van is still your number one guy."

Hanley nodded. "He remains my lead technician because you trained him well and he's totally dedicated. It would be hard to replace him."

Minutes later Morton arrived. After being briefed on what Lawson needed, he said, "It shouldn't be any problem. We'll start by checking the organization charts of the four companies you're interested in to see if they have a position for that function. If they don't, we'll monitor the information exchanges of the senior executives to see who they're using. Either way we'll tap the individual's phones and monitor their computers to see how they operate. I'll get a couple of people on the project as soon as possible and give you a report in a couple days."

"Thanks, Van," Lawson said. "As always I'm indebted to you."

Morton shook his head. "No, sir, I'm indebted to you for steering me into this career. And as you know, I love my job."

Lawson nodded. "Catch you later, Van."

After he left, Hanley said, "What about the others on your list?"

Lawson shook his head. "I'll defer those. They're relatively unimportant and I think your people have enough on their plate monitoring the Tea Party crowd."

"Do you need us to change the minds of any minority reviewers of Thurston's book?"

Lawson smiled. "That won't be necessary. So far the reviews have been uniformly good and the book promises to be another best seller. So we're off and running."

Hanley nodded. "Do you like our chances?"

Lawson smiled. "So far everything is going according to plan. But . . . and it's a big but . . . we won't get over the top unless Thurston's story gets to the big screen. So I'll be a bit anxious until Morton gives me something to work with."

"Relax, you know damn well he will. So what's your plan when he identifies a contact for you?"

"That depends on who and what the contact is. But regardless, I'll be going to Hollywood as Thurston's agent."

Hanley raised his eyebrows. "And you'll be going with an unlimited expense account, I assume."

"Yeah, something like that."

Hanley shook his head. "Then be careful you don't get sucked into Hollywood's notorious whirlpool of decadence."

Lawson laughed. "What the hell are you talking about, Jack. I'm a little old to be mixing with the jet set crowd."

"Hey, Terry, there are Hollywood moguls older than you that get laid twice a day."

Lawson shook his head. "What the hell difference does it make, Jack? I'm going out there on business.'"

Hanley smiled. "I remember when you used to go to Bangkok and Saigon on business. It seems you always found plenty of time for sex on those trips."

Lawson frowned. "That was long ago and far away, and I was single then. This is an entirely different type of business trip and an entirely different time in history—and I'm married. You should keep in mind that the vast majority of those in Hollywood are businesspeople that have families and lead respectable lives. Besides, I'll be going there on a mission of extreme importance. End of discussion."

"Excuse me for trying to help."

"You're excused. Now a little advice for you—stop reading the tabloids and check out the real world from time to time. With that said, I'm about to depart, so would you be kind enough to let me know when Van has something?"

Hanley nodded. "That goes without saying. And for your information I've checked out the real world and I don't much care for it."

CHAPTER 24

▼

Two Days Later, CIA Headquarters, Langley, Virginia: Lawson walked into Hanley's office and said, "Good morning, Jack, good morning, Van. I got here as quickly as I could."

"Good morning, Terry," Hanley said. "I think you'll like what Van has for you."

"Do I need to take notes?"

"No, you'll get a complete briefing package. Go ahead, Van."

Morton nodded and said, "I think we have exactly what you were looking for in a contact. Her name is Brenda Carpenter. She's thirty-seven years old and single. She grew up in Poughkeepsie, New York, and graduated from Vassar with a degree in journalism. Her first job was with the *New York Times* as a trainee in the news department. Five years and several promotions later she was reviewing and rating potential best sellers. In doing that she developed a reputation for writing insightful and critical reviews. So it wasn't long before she was lured to Hollywood by a second-tier movie production company that was looking for someone to help them find stories with movie potential. Two years later she was recruited by one of Hollywood's largest production companies—one of your five—to work for the VP of creative development, reviewing screenplays and books. Are we okay so far?"

Lawson nodded. "I like what I'm hearing, Van. So give me the rest of the story."

"Yes, sir. Apparently Ms. Carpenter was very successful since she held that key position until two years ago. What happened then isn't entirely clear. However, we know it involved some disagreement with her boss, probably about salary. We suspect that was the case because she left and formed her own consulting firm which specializes in discovering literary work with screen potential. Last year she paid tax on just over a million."

Lawson nodded. "You're right, Van, Ms. Carpenter is just what I was looking for. Do you have her contact information?"

"Yes, sir, it's all in the package. We have the addresses of her house in Santa Monica and her office on Wilshire Boulevard in Beverly Hills. We also have all her phone numbers, including her cell."

"Good. Have you picked up anything that might be useful in doing business with her?"

"Only that she's having an intimate relationship with another woman. If you want we can go into full surveillance mode to pick up more."

Lawson nodded. "That would be helpful. I'll probably be going out there in a few days, so whatever you can dig up before then would be appreciated."

"No problem, and if you want, we can continue to monitor her communications while you're there."

Lawson smiled. "That would be excellent. I'll take everything you can give me, no matter how trivial it might seem. You never know what will be useful."

Morton nodded. "I'll leave it to Mr. Hanley to make whatever arrangements we'll need for real time communications."

Hanley smiled. "And I'll ask Van to tell me what he recommends."

Morton nodded. "I'll include the gear we'll need to effect those communications. At minimum we'll use mobiles to exchange text messages."

"Sounds good, and thanks again, Van," Lawson said. "I'll let you know what the travel plans are no later than tomorrow."

Later that day: The Harrisons greeted Lawson and ushered him into their living room. "Would you like something to drink?" Jennifer said."

Lawson nodded. "A vodka tonic would really hit the spot."

When Jennifer left to fix his drink, Harrison said, "How was traffic on Ninety-Five?"

"Apparently, I came at a good time—it was tolerable. So how are you guys doing?"

"Oh, we're fine, just a little anxious about your trip."

Lawson nodded. "So am I, but I'm also optimistic. Jack's people will be feeding me real-time intelligence on my contact's movements and conversations. And if I can't get it done with that kind of help, I should hang it up."

At that moment Jennifer appeared with Lawson's drink. "Hang what up?" she asked.

Lawson smiled. "That's a sports euphemism—the 'it' is a jockstrap."

Jennifer laughed. "In that case let's hope you don't have to hang 'it' up. Now when do you plan to travel?"

"Two days from now, unless I hear that my contact won't be available."

"Do you need me to make your airline and hotel reservations?"

"No, that won't be necessary. Phil's people are taking care of all that. The legend they developed for me is that of Justin Hartley, an agent of best-selling authors. The agency, Hartley Associates, is an office suite in Bethesda on Wisconsin Avenue. To establish the legend they're providing me with Hartley's background documents, business cards, and a platinum American Express card. The AMEX card is nice in that it'll enable me to sustain the legend of Hartley being a very successful agent who flies first-class and stays at upscale hotels like the Beverly Hilton."

Jennifer shook her head. "Same old Tiger. You never miss an opportunity to go first-class do you?"

"Come on Jennifer, you know damn well it's part of the job. Besides, it doesn't hurt to walk a little in the enemies' shoes to better understand why they're so screwed up."

Harrison smiled. "It sounds as if you've wrapped this package pretty tightly. So what do you need from us?"

"I just need your blessing for the op. Oh, and a couple of preset disposables so I can contact you while I'm there."

Harrison smiled. "It sounds like you and the others have this worked out very nicely, so it's a go. We'll give you a few phones but you won't need to use them unless there's an emergency. Phil and Jack will keep us informed of your progress."

Jennifer smiled. "Try not to go Hollywood on us, Tiger . . . and good luck."

CHAPTER 25

▼

Lawson's flight from Dulles to LAX on United's new Boeing 787 Dreamliner was smooth and uneventful. And the six-hour flight was just long enough for the first-class passengers to consume two meals and several glasses of champagne. Lawson was relaxed enough that the twenty-minute wait for his baggage didn't bother him. Nor did the ten-minute wait for a cab, nor the thirty-minute drive to the Beverly Hilton. He arrived there feeling good enough to give the gregarious driver a fifteen-dollar tip.

Lawson followed the bellman and his luggage inside the Hilton to the registration desk. The desk clerk looked up and said, "May I help you, sir?"

"Yes, I'm Justin Hartley and I have a reservation. Do you need a confirmation number?"

The desk clerk shook his head and said, "No, sir." Then after a few moments of interacting with his computer, the clerk said, "Welcome to the Beverly Hilton, Mr. Hartley. We have you in a King Executive Suite on the fifth floor. Will that be satisfactory?"

Lawson nodded. "I'm sure it will be. If it's not, I'll let you know."

The clerk smiled and said, "Now then, if you'll just sign this registration form, your bellman will take you to room 514. Enjoy your stay, sir."

Lawson nodded his thanks and followed the young bellman to the elevator. Three minutes later he was in suite 514. After the bellman placed his suitcase on the luggage stand and his hang-up bag in the closet, Lawson handed him a ten-dollar bill. As soon as the surprised and smiling bellman left, Lawson checked out the suite. He decided it was one of the nicest hotel accommodations he had had since staying at the Grand Hotel in Taipei. The living room was comfortably furnished and of sufficient size to accommodate upward of ten for cocktails. The equally spacious king bedroom was also beautifully furnished. The bath had both a Jacuzzi bath and a stall shower. He was sure he would be more than comfortable for whatever amount of time was needed to complete his mission.

Lawson took just a few minutes to unpack and put away his clothes and equipment. With that done, he reset his watch to Pacific time and noted that it was only 1415. That meant Brenda Carpenter would likely be in her office. Lawson retrieved one of the smart mobile phones Morton had given him, entered Carpenter's office number and hit Talk. Moments later a youngish-sounding female voice said, "Carpenter Associates, how may I help you?"

"I'd like to speak with Ms. Carpenter please."

"I'm sorry, sir, but she's out of the office with a client."

"I see. My name is Justin Hartley and I just arrived from Washington, DC. I'm the agent for Sidney Thurston who's most recent novel *Saving Democracy* is a best seller. It's a property I'm sure Ms. Carpenter will agree has great movie potential. So I'd like an appointment to meet with her and give her a copy of the book."

"Yes, Mr. Hartley, I'll give her your message. How may we reach you?"

"I'm staying at the Beverly Hilton, room 514."

"Very good, sir, we'll get back to you as soon as possible."

Lawson went to the minibar and retrieved the makings of a vodka tonic. When the drink was assembled, he got comfortable in a lounge chair and tuned in ESPN on the widescreen TV. He was pleased to see that ESPN was broadcasting the Australian open tennis matches from Melbourne. After an hour of watching tennis, he picked up the second mobile Morton had given him and hit the number-one fast-dial button. Two rings later the call was answered. "Morton here, how are you doing, sir?"

"I'm fine, Van. I called Carpenter's office over an hour ago, but no call back as yet."

Lawson could hear Morton chuckle, then say, "You'll get a call in about an hour from now informing you of an office appointment at ten tomorrow morning."

"How did you get that?"

"The woman you spoke to in the office called Carpenter's cell and gave her your message. She wants to see you but told her secretary to wait a couple hours before calling you back in order to avoid seeming anxious."

"Good work, Van. I'll let you know how tomorrow's meeting goes. By the way I'm in room 514 at the Beverly Hilton."

Again Morton chuckled. "I knew what room you were in, and you don't need to keep me informed. We'll be hearing everything we need to know. Oh, and don't forget, anytime you're with her have your other mobile in record mode."

"Thanks for the reminder, Van. But I have to tell you, you're getting a little scary. Knowing what you're capable of forces me to stay on my best behavior."

"Don't worry, sir. What happens in Hollywood stays in Hollywood. Good luck tomorrow, sir," Morton said before disconnecting.

Lawson checked his watch again and saw he still had more than an hour to wait. He trusted the minibar would help make the wait tolerable.

After breakfast the next morning Lawson donned a dark pinstriped suit, red foulard tie, and black wingtip shoes. *Very professional looking*, he thought. He then packed his briefcase with two copies of *Saving Democracy*, two pages of reviews, and his Daytimer appointment book. The recording mobile went in the left inside pocket of his suit jacket. His business card holder went in the other inside pocket.

His plan was to catch a cab at 0945. He figured that since the Beverly Hilton and Carpenter's office were both on Wilshire Boulevard, fifteen minutes would be sufficient time for him to arrive on schedule. He was right. The cab dropped him off at two minutes before 1000.

He rode the elevator to the fourth floor and quickly found Suite 402. When he entered he was greeted by an attractive blonde he estimated to in her early twenties. "Good morning, Mr. Hartley," she said. "Ms. Carpenter will be with you in just a few minutes. Would you care for something to drink while you're waiting?"

"Black coffee would be fine, thank you."

After getting his coffee, Lawson opened the briefcase, took out one of Thurston's books, and began to read. He had only gotten to the bottom of page two when the door to Carpenter's office opened and she came out. As Lawson stood, she extended her hand and said, "I'm Brenda Carpenter."

While they shook hands, Lawson said, "And I'm Justin Hartley. Very nice to meet you, Brenda."

She smiled. "The pleasure is mine, Justin. Please come in."

Lawson quickly put Thurston's book back in the briefcase, closed it, and followed Carpenter into her office.

"Please take a seat," she said and motioned to one of the two chairs in front of her desk. "Now then what can I do for you?"

Lawson retrieved a business card and handed it to her. "I represent Burns and Solomon the publishers of Sidney Thurston's most recent book, *Saving Democracy.* As you may or may not know, it's currently on the best seller list." He then handed her the sheet of laudatory reviews and said, "As you can see, the book has been embraced by a wide range of reviewers, most of whom used the words *compelling* and *riveting* to describe Thurston's story. And I'm here today to persuade you that the book would make a great movie."

Carpenter nodded. "I appreciate your getting right to the point, Justin. Now tell me why it would make a great movie."

Lawson smiled. "Let's start with the fact that it's a compelling story, a political thriller that's both entertaining and informative. Thurston wrote it as a novel, for reasons I'm sure you understand, but it's based entirely on actual people and current events. Some refer to that type of novel as faction—part fact and part fiction.'"

Carpenter thought for a moment before saying, "What kind of actual people and events are we talking about?"

Lawson nodded. "I'm sure when you read it that will be abundantly clear. But for the moment let's just say the people are public figures—mainly congressmen and high-ranking government officials. Somewhat less recognizable are the power brokers responsible for the corruption that's eroding our democracy. The real events are, for the most part, the perverse congressional obstructionism that is currently costing our country dearly. Oh, and Thurston also reveals the criminal and sexual misbehavior of several congressional leaders."

Carpenter smiled. "That's fine, a little spice in the soup never hurts. I'll be honest, you do make the story sound intriguing. But I'm curious about the other reasons you think it would make a commercially successful movie."

Lawson nodded. "Well, first of all, the movie would be based on a widely read, highly acclaimed, and controversial novel, which means there will be a relatively large audience-in-waiting for the movie version. Another reason is that the movie could be produced at minimal cost."

"Why is that?"

"Mainly because Thurston wrote the novel so it could easily be converted into a screenplay that has a small cast and only a few location settings."

Carpenter nodded. "That makes sense. But why are you bringing the book to me?"

Lawson smiled. "Because I'm confident you could facilitate getting Thurston's story made into a movie. I appreciate the difficulty of getting a book, even a best seller, in front of major producers. That would be especially true for an outsider like me. So I'm sure getting it done requires key contacts, which I believe you have."

Carpenter smiled. "You're right, I do. But my contacts expect a little incentive pay for their cooperation. The fact is every wheel in the production machinery needs to be greased."

Lawson nodded. "I know and that's not a problem. Burns and Solomon have a great deal of grease. From what you're telling me it seems a general contractor is needed to ensure all the greased functionaries work harmoniously."

Carpenter laughed. "I've never heard it described quite that way before, but you're right. So if you hire me, I'll be that facilitating general contractor."

"That's why I'm here. You have the reputation of being someone who can take a promising property and do what's necessary to get it into theatres across the country."

Carpenter nodded. "That's very flattering, Justin, but justified. I have had my share of successes."

Lawson smiled. "And that's why I'm prepared to make your next success rather lucrative."

Carpenter cocked her head. "That got my attention, Justin, because it's just what we facilitators like to hear. But as you said earlier, the process begins with a promising property. On the surface it looks like Thurston's book is just such a property, but I'll have to make that determination myself."

"Lawson nodded. "Of course, that's understood." He then retrieved two copies of Thurston's book from his briefcase and said, "And that's why I brought these copies of *Saving Democracy*—so you can see for yourself."

"Thank you. I'm glad you brought two copies because I have an associate who will be helping me make that determination." Carpenter then hit the intercom and told her secretary to have Martina come to her office.

Two minutes later a striking brunette came through the door, prompting Carpenter to say, "Justin, this is my associate, Martina Gomez."

Gomez flashed a dazzling smile and said, "Very nice to meet you, Justin." She then took the seat next to him. *God, she's beautiful,* he thought.

Carpenter handed her a copy of the book and said, "Justin is representing Sidney Thurston's publisher and he makes a good case for the book being convertible to a successful movie. I'd like you to review it and see if you agree."

Gomez nodded and said, "How soon do you need me to do that?"

"Since Justin came all the way from Washington, I'm sure he'd like it done as soon as practicable. Am I correct, Justin?"

Lawson nodded. "Given the cost of living in the LA area, I'm inclined to say yes."

Gomez smiled and said, "I have nothing else on my plate at the moment, so I can start right away. I should be finished by noon tomorrow."

Carpenter nodded. "Thank you, Martina. Unfortunately it will take me a little longer. Nevertheless we should have a preliminary assessment for you by close of business tomorrow."

"That would be wonderful," Lawson said. "So would it be possible for us to discuss your evaluation over dinner tomorrow evening?"

Carpenter nodded. "I believe so. What did you have in mind?"

"For years I've heard about Wolfgang Puck's Spago Restaurant, and would like to try it. Would dinning there be suitable?"

Carpenter smiled. "Indeed, eating at Spago is always delightful."

"Shall I make the reservation for three at eight?

Gomez looked quizzically at Carpenter who turned to Lawson and said, "Yes, that would be fine."

Lawson smiled. "Good. I'll call you to confirm the reservation and time. And if you have any questions before then, just call me at the hotel."

CHAPTER 26

▼

The Following Day: After breakfast Lawson returned to his room, broke out his iPad, and went to the Spago webpage. He was surprised to learn that in addition to the one on Rodeo Drive, there was a new one on North Canyon Drive just off Wilshire Boulevard. After deciding on the new one, he copied down the information he needed. He called the listed number and had no problem making a reservation for that evening. With that done, he called Carpenter's office and informed them that the reservation was made in his name for 8:00 p.m.

A bit later he contacted Morton to inform him of the reservation and to see if he had gotten any intelligence on Martina Gomez. Morton said he had, that she was living with Carpenter in Santa Monica and that she was a UCLA graduate and an aspiring actress. Morton apologized for not having more but promised to keep investigating.

Lawson spent much of the day touring the Los Angeles area with a private tour guide, a graduate student at USC. The guide proved to be both entertaining and knowledgeable about the places he took Lawson—well worth the sixty dollars an hour he charged. There were two places they visited that were especially impressive for Lawson. The first was the ultra exclusive Bellaire community where all the megastars and ultra-wealthy celebrities live. While riding through Bellaire, Lawson was awestruck by the size and elegance of the homes.

The second locale Lawson found interesting was the J. Paul Getty Museum, which was perched high up in the Hollywood hills in the Pacific Palisades. He was immediately impressed with the main building for two reasons. First, because it was a copy of an architecturally magnificent ancient Greek villa and second because the view from there was breathtaking. But the best was yet to come. When he went inside the museum, he was treated to a stellar collection of early Greek art, which he learned was priceless. He also learned that the Getty Museum was valued at 1.2 billion dollars, making it the wealthiest museum in the world. After spending more than an hour in the museum admiring the art, Lawson went outside and was treated to a spectacular panoramic view of the Los Angeles area, including the adjacent hills that were dotted with homes of the rich and famous.

Later that day, Lawson enjoyed tours of Venice, where he saw the canals and the carefree hippies along the beach; Hollywood, where he saw the Chinese Theatre and the Walk of Fame; and Pasadena, where he toured the route of the New Year's Day Rose Parade and the coliseum where the Rose Bowl is played. He found each of those locales interesting, but not as much so as the Getty. When he finished touring, he had run up a bill of $180. He felt he had gotten his money's worth, so when he was dropped him off at the hotel, he gave his graduate student guide two one hundred dollar bills. This earned him a commercial-sized smile.

It was near four when Lawson got back to his room. Feeling a bit tired, he quickly scanned a copy of *USA Today* and took a brief nap. Afterward he contacted Morton for an intelligence update. When Morton had nothing new to tell him, he went down to the bar for a martini and nuts. Shortly after he took a seat at the bar, an attractive young woman came in and seductively slid onto the bar stool next to him. After a few minutes of get-acquainted chitchat, she asked Lawson if he would like her company for the evening. When he declined, she quickly left.

After finishing his second martini and a bowl of nuts, Lawson returned to his room to prepare for dinner. After a shower and touchup shave, he raided the minibar for the makings of a vodka tonic. With drink in hand and thirty minutes to kill, he turned on TV to watch the evening news. Feeling a bit contentious, he tuned in arch conservative Rupert Mudock's primary propaganda factory,

Fox News, or Faux News as he liked to call it. He then watched with amusement as a mini-parade of radical commentators did exaggerated parodies of themselves mouthing a litany of lies and venomously attacking the president. *The same old crap*, he thought and turned off the TV. It was time to get dressed.

When Lawson had made his Spago reservation, he inquired about the appropriate dress for the evening. He was told that the better-dressed men wore sport coats and open necked shirts and no ties. That prompted him to wear a blue blazer, gray trousers, and a blue pinstriped oxford button-down shirt, open at the neck

At 0745 he went to the lobby to catch a cab. When the doorman asked his destination, Lawson said, "The Spago Restaurant."

"The old one, or the new one?"

"The new one."

"Yes, sir, I have a cab coming now."

When the cab stopped, the doorman opened the rear cab door for Lawson, who handed him a three-dollar tip. The doorman then went to the front window and said, "The Spago on North Canyon Drive."

The driver nodded and pulled away. Ten minutes later he pulled up in front of the restaurant. After checking the meter, he quickly ran around to open Lawson's door. "That'll be twelve dollars, sir," he said.

Lawson nodded, thanked him for the ride, and handed him a twenty.

As he walked away he heard the surprised driver say, "Thank you very much, sir."

Inside, Lawson was greeted by an attractive young hostess who said, "May I help you?"

Lawson nodded. "My name is Hartley. I have a reservation for a party of three at eight."

"Your guests are already seated, sir," she said while beckoning a waiter who was hovering nearby. "His name is Paul—he'll show you to your table."

Paul nodded to Lawson and said, "This way, Mr. Hartley."

He then led Lawson to a round table in the far corner of the room. As the two approached, Carpenter stood and said, "Good evening, Justin. I hope you don't mind that we arrived a bit early, but

I wanted to ensure we had this table—it's a favorite of mine. I think you'll see why in a moment."

Lawson smiled, "Good evening, and thank you for getting this table. I can see it's well located. Now then, please sit down."

Paul held the chair at the far side of the table for Lawson, then asked, "May I get you a drink, sir. The ladies are having Cosmo martinis."

Lawson nodded. "The same for me please." After Paul moved away, Lawson said, "Do you two come here often?"

Carpenter smiled. "Yes, as often as possible. It's a prime place to see and to be seen."

Lawson nodded. "And who or what should I expect to see this evening?"

Carpenter cocked her head and said, "There are all kinds of possibilities since most everyone in the industry comes here at one time or another. On any given evening you can expect to see two or three stars and half a dozen or so Academy Award nominees and winners."

Lawson nodded. "I'll try to stay alert, but you may have to point them out to me. So will Wolfgang Puck be among the luminaries we see tonight?"

"I don't expect so."

"Do you know him?"

"Just well enough to get this table whenever I want."

Lawson laughed. "Did you ever make it to one of his post Oscar bashes?"

Carpenter smiled and shook her head. "I was never invited, but I did crash one a couple of years ago. A celebrity acquaintance of mine who was a bit high on coke snuck me in. After about fifteen minutes of being ignored, I left."

"Do you have many celebrity acquaintances?"

"Just a few, most of my friends and acquaintances are people who work behind the scenes in the industry. In general they're more interesting people."

Lawson nodded. "How about you Martina, do you have any notables in your address book?"

Gomez smiled, shook her head, and said, "Not really. I'm something of a newcomer to the movie business. But thanks to Brenda I'm learning how the industry functions from the bottom up. I've studied acting and have gotten a few bit parts, but I'm putting that ambition on hold until I have more experience."

At that moment Paul reappeared and served the drinks. "Shall I give you more time to look over the menu?"

Everyone nodded.

Lawson raised his glass and said, "Here's to a pleasant evening."

Carpenter and Gomez clicked glasses with Lawson and repeated the toast."

When there was a lull in the conversation, Lawson said, "Before we discuss business, I'd like to get better acquainted. Brenda, I know you graduated from Vassar with honors, so I'd like to ask if you're as conservative as was most of the Vassar crowd?"

Carpenter laughed. "Hardly, unlike my pampered classmates from Westchester, I was a full scholarship student and had to work to earn spending money. So I'm the antithesis of a conservative. And if you identify at all with Sidney Thurston's writing, you aren't either."

Lawson laughed. "That's true, and that's why I'm so passionate about getting Thurston's story to the masses. And with that said, it seems we've gotten to the business aspect of this evening rather quickly."

Carpenter nodded. "Which is fine, because I'm not a games player, I'm a pragmatic businesswoman. Since Martina and I agree that *Saving Democracy* is a viable property, we're prepared do everything we can to get it into production—and do so as soon as possible. But making that happen will require upfront money."

"How much are we talking about?"

"A hundred thousand."

Lawson nodded. "That's not a showstopper because the people I represent have me on a rather long leash."

Carpenter smiled. "Good. First thing in the morning I'll have a contract drawn up for you to see and sign. It'll spell out exactly what we intend to do and what it will cost. We're flexible, so most every provision in the contract will be negotiable, except for one."

"And what is that?"

"The one-hundred-thousand-dollar retainer I mentioned. We'll need that to initiate the project and manage it full-time."

Lawson nodded. "Apparently we have a deal. And I must confess, I'm looking forward to working with you. Now then, I believe we've concluded our business meeting, so let's get something to eat. Is there anything special on the menu that you would recommend?"

Carpenter smiled. You probably won't recognize too many of the menu items. Most of them were created by Wolfgang and are referred to as California cuisine—tasty but healthy."

"Given that," Lawson said, "I'll have whatever you're having."

CHAPTER 27

▼

The Following Day, Brenda Carpenter's Office: "Good morning, Justin," Carpenter said. "I hope you enjoyed your evening at Spago's."

Lawson nodded. "The evening was fine, but I think my stomach felt a bit deprived. There's no doubt California Cuisine is healthy, but in my gut's opinion, it comes up short of being filling. But it was no problem, the minibar got me through the night. So here I am, ready to seal the deal on our business arrangement. Is the contract ready?"

Carpenter nodded as she handed Lawson a three-page document and said, "This is the nonbinding contract I described last night. It spells out stepwise what I intend to do to get Thurston's story produced as a movie. The only thing required of Hartley Associates at this time is to pay my company a retainer of one hundred thousand dollars. Look it over and let me know if you have any questions."

Lawson nodded. "This will take a few minutes, so may I have another cup of coffee please?"

"Certainly, Janice will get it for you."

Three minutes later, Lawson said, "I see that your primary path to a leading producer is through a screenwriter. Why is that?"

Carpenter smiled. "Because they're the key to attracting a producer's attention—every producer is constantly looking for a strong screenplay to work with. And each of the screenwriters I intend to solicit has written a screenplay that one or more producers have embraced. In addition, they've all received recognition at Oscar time, and each has worked with one or more of the best producers."

Lawson nodded. "That's good, thank you." Two minutes later he said, "I'm satisfied with the contract and ready to sign."

"So you're comfortable covering all our out-of-pocket expenses and awarding us a hundred-thousand-dollar completion bonus, right?"

Lawson just nodded.

"Good. We'll be signing two copies. I'll sign on the first line of each and you on the second line. Martina will notarize both copies on the third line."

When the signing was over, Carpenter handed Lawson his copy and said, "The contract will go into effect as soon as I receive the retainer."

Lawson nodded. "I'll arrange a wire transfer. You should have the money sometime today."

Carpenter smiled. "In that case, lunch is on me."

When he got back to the hotel, Lawson contacted Morton and gave him Carpenter's bank account number and her bank's routing number. Morton told him the money would be transferred within the hour. He then informed Lawson that Carpenter had just made a phone call to someone named Phil, and told him she had a book she wanted him to read because she believes it will make a profitable movie. Hearing that, Lawson said, "Have you had a chance to check out his phone number?"

"Yes, the number belongs to a Philip Warren but that's all that we know at this time. Do you want us to monitor his calls?"

"For the time being just record the calls between him and Carpenter, and when you have a chance, check out his résumé."

"Okay, is there anything else you need?"

"Just tell your boss I'll be back in Virginia tomorrow evening."

"Will do, sir . . . talk to you later."

When Lawson returned to the hotel after having lunch with Carpenter, he used one of the Harrisons' disposable cell phones to call them. It was John who answered. "Hello, Terry, I understand you've been having a grand time in LA."

"You might say that John, but it's really been serious work. Fortunately Hollywood is loaded with attractive women, so the work has been tolerable. But the bottom line is that Operation Movie Time is off to a fast start and looks rather promising."

"Good work, Terry. After you're back and reconciled with Lan, we'll have a little welcome home party."

"For your information, John, I've called Lan at least twice a day since I've been here."

"Did you mention all the attractive women you were forced to work with?"

"Yes, and I told her she was more beautiful than any of them."

Harrison laughed. "That's good, Terry. I see you've been studying the domestic survival guide."

"That's just instinct, John. I'll call you when I'm back . . . and rested."

"Thanks, Terry."

CHAPTER 28

▼

Five Days Later at the Harrisons': The atmosphere was unmistakably celebratory as the phantom patriots finished off a second bottle of champagne. When Jennifer noticed Lawson facetiously inverting his flute, she told her husband to open another bottle. An observer of this celebration most likely would have commented that no Fifth Avenue party or Great Gatsby gala ever rivaled what was happening that evening at the Harrisons'. When the seemingly endless toasts were becoming more and more slurred, Jennifer clicked her glass for attention and announced that everyone should follow her into the secured meeting room. She added that they could bring their glasses if they wished. Most did so.

Once everyone was seated, Harrison said. "Please keep in mind that tonight we're celebrating a major milestone in our quiet revolution. However, we still have promises to keep and miles to go before we sleep. That is to say, we still have some heavy lifting to do before our revolution is a success. Now then, with that said, I'd like Terry to report on our two ongoing operations—Operation Movie Time and Operation TBT. Terry . . ."

Lawson smiled and said, "Please bear with me as I try to make this coherent. As for Movie Time I think you all know that we're on track to have a movie made based on Thurston's book. A noted screenwriter named Phillip Warren is writing the screenplay and he's directly connected to one of Hollywood's leading producers."

Hanley raised a finger and said, "We're continuing to monitor the calls being made by our facilitator in Hollywood and by Phillip

Warren. So I'm pleased to confirm what Terry just said. It's going to happen because everyone involved expects to make a great deal of money from this movie."

"Thanks, Phil," Lawson said. "And we're among those making money from it. We've already made a million from selling the copyright. Then, after the movie is released, we'll be getting 5 percent of the movie's net profits. Of course that's never as much as it should be because the studio accountants are prone to cook the books a bit. Okay, that's it for Movie Time. Now as for Operation TBT, it's going as well as could be expected at this time. Most encouraging is the fact that Democratic fund-raising in Texas is currently keeping pace with Republican fund-raising. That means progressives are seeing women and Hispanics mobilizing, and that there's a decent possibility of capturing the governor's mansion. Thurston's book is now in the hands of the Democratic leadership there and should have a positive influence on how they manage the upcoming election. I hope that's enough information for now since I'm a bit light-headed and thick-tongued."

Harrison nodded, "I understood most of what you said, so well done. But again I would remind everyone that we still have work to do and not to be complacent. Now I hate to end this evening on a sad note, but we're out of champagne. Given that, the best I can do is caution you to either drive carefully or crash here for the night. Remember, we still have miles to go."

EPILOGUE

▼

In the ensuing months the phantom patriots remained engaged in their quiet revolution in differing ways. Lawson was the most visibly active. As Sidney Thurston's agent and spokesperson, he was asked on occasions to appear on television to defend Thurston's contentious prose and his motivation. Lawson always relished those opportunities because his conservative interrogators had so little to say in the way of rebuttal. At other times Lawson would go to Hollywood to observe firsthand the making of *Saving Democracy*. He continued to be impressed with what he saw. For Operation TBT he and Lan frequently traveled to Texas to meet with Charlie Garcia and receive progress reports on their Turn Texas Blue movement. On most occasions they were pleased with what they saw and heard. It seemed to them measurable progress was being made.

Jack Hanley remained proactive in monitoring the misbehavior of those on Capitol Hill. He did so in order to funnel the information to those who found it useful. He also monitored the key players who were making Thurston's movie to ensure they were progressing effectively.

Phil Martin remained perpetually busy with his day job, especially since so little was being resolved in the Middle East. Members of his staff, however, found time to place entertaining and revelatory videos on YouTube. Their best effort in that regard was the one Lawson had recommended, which figuratively stripped the president of the NRA naked. Martin's people also whipped up a number of graphically exquisite ads eviscerating the Tea Party. They also kept a light on in Lawson's Hartley & Associates office in Bethesda.

The Harrisons remained in seclusion while closely watching the unfolding of progressive campaigns nationwide. To stay current and informed they monitored postings on the social networks and read informative periodicals such as *Time* and *The Nation*. Their evenings began watching Comedy Central's *Daily Show* and, a little later, MSNBC's evening shows. On one occasion they were less than satisfied with what they were seeing and hearing, so they asked Hanley to check whether the DNC and DCCC were heeding Thurston's advice. When Hanley reported that the leadership was not actively distributing campaign guidance nationwide, Harrison gave him a green light to blackmail them.

While the patriots stayed busy with the build up to the 2014 elections, John Barlow was luxuriating in Provence in the south of France. His days were spent in Nice or Cap d'Antibe or Monico. Fortunately he found more satisfaction in the museums of Nice and the white sand beaches of the Cote d'Azure than he did in the casino at Monte Carlo. For Barlow life was good. His book was selling like hotcakes and his Swiss bank account was growing by leaps and bounds. But the best was yet to come. Six weeks before the November elections, the movie *Saving Democracy* hit screens across the country. It would prove to be a lynchpin for arresting the downward spiral of democracy, morality, and social justice in America. In a later time, Sidney Thurston would be remembered as the patriot that saved our country from the death grip of the rich and powerful.